NECROTECH

MAGITECH LEGACY BOOK 3

CHRIS FOX

CHRIS FOX WRITES LLC

The Magitech Chronicles

Buckle up, because you're about to enter *The Magitech Chronicles*. If you like *Necrotech*, we have a complete seven-book prequel series with an ending already available.

Our pen & paper RPG successfully Kickstarted and the game will be live on July 30th, 2020. You can learn more at magitechchronicles.com or our Magitech Chronicles World Anvil page.

We've got maps, lore, character sheets, and a free set of rules you can use to generate your own character.

I hope you enjoy!

-Chris

THE MAGITECH CHRONICLES
CHARACTER SHEET

NAME: Jerek

RACE: Human

ARCHETYPE: True Mage

PATH: Relic Hunter

HIT POINTS	SPELL POINTS	INITIATIVE
20 20	21 21	3(6)

⚖ ATTRIBUTES

All Attributes begin play at 2. You have 5 points to spend, and no attribute can be higher than 5

Agility	3 (6)
Fortitude	2 (5)
Strength	2 (5)
Reason	5
Intuition	2
Will	4
Appearance	2
Charisma	3

DEFENSES 🛡

Brace, Skepticism & Dodge begin at 1. You have 5 points to spend between them. Brace cannot be higher than Fort. Skepticism cannot be higher than Will. Dodge cannot be higher than Agility

1	:	Brace
4	:	Skepticism
3	:	Dodge
9	:	Armor
3 Fire	:	Resistances
3 Dream	:	Resistances
9	:	Resistances
	:	Resistances

SKILL	RANK	ATTRIBUTE	MASTERY	ROLL
Spellcasting	3	5	N	8
Arcana	4	5	Y	9
History and Lore	5	5	Y	10
Perception	3	2	Y	5
Ranged	4	3/5	Y	9
Negotiation	3	3	N	6

ATTACKS & COMBAT SPELLS	DAMAGE	ACCURACY	DEFENSE	ROLL
Heka Aten Fire Bolt	4/3	2	SKEP	10
Heka Aten Void Bolt	5	3	SKEP	11

ABILITIES & SPELLS	EFFECT
Decipher	Translate any language
Tomb Robber	Edge when using ektimagus
Dream Bolt	
Fire Bolt	
Invest Strength	
Invest Charisma	
Perfect Perception	Cannot be lied to. Always see.

ARMOR	A/R	EFFECT
Heka Aten Spellarmor	9/9	

CIVILIZATION	ASPECT	BENEFIT
Fire Magic	Fire	3 pool, 3 fire resistance
Dream Magic	Dream	3 pool, 3 dream resistance
Life Magic	Life	3 Pool, 3 life resistance

PERKS	FLAWS
Slippery Mofo (+1 Dodge)	Skipped Leg Day (-1 Strength)

THE MAGITECH CHRONICLES
CHARACTER SHEET

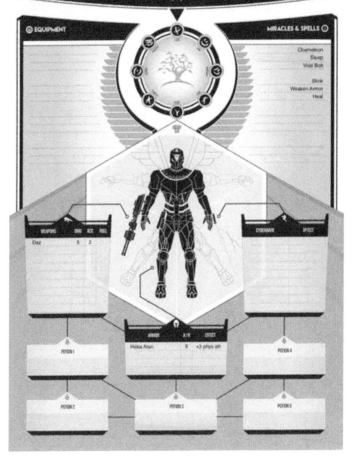

EQUIPMENT

MIRACLES & SPELLS

Chameleon
Sleep
Void Bolt

Blink
Weaken Armor
Heal

WEAPONS	DMG	XCR	PIERCE
Dez	5	2	

CYBERWARE | EFFECT

ARMOR	A/R	EFFECT
Hexa Alvin	9	+3 phys att

POTION 1

POTION 2

POTION 3

POTION 4

POTION 5

PREVIOUSLY ON

You know that annoying feeling when you pick up a sequel and have to make that monumental decision? How well do you remember the previous book in the series? Do you dive right in or do a reread?

I always tell myself I'm going to do the reread, but I can never wait and so I jump right into the latest book. Sometimes I can't remember what happened, so my solution for my own books is to write a Previously On, delivered just like the recap before most of our favorite TV shows.

Here's what happened in Hatchling, told from Jerek's perspective.

Last time on Magitech Legacy...

.   .   .

Hey there again, uh...you. So, I'm supposed to recap my amazing adventures. Here's the TL;DR version.

After Kemet blew up, we inherited some big problems. We needed supplies, and we needed to find a way to pay off the very Inurans who'd destroyed our world.

The minister charged me with relic hunting one of the derelict Great Ships, and I chose the *Flame of Knowledge*. Knowledge is power, right?

Well, the ship wasn't empty. In fact, they were expecting us, and had been for, like, 9,000 years. They even had a prophecy.

We fulfilled it, and got out of there with a hold full of knowledge scales. That wasn't the real treasure though. We exchanged our junky version of the *Remora* for the pristine version that existed thousands of years ago.

After we got off the *Flame* we learned the Inurans, under the command of someone named Jolene, had assaulted the *Word* and were trying to seize control.

We stopped them by bringing in the Confederacy.

I captured their leader, a guy by the name of Bortel.

Wow, the short version is pretty long.

The longer version...

The story began with us flying through the Vagrant Fleet to the *Flame of Knowledge*. As you'd expect, we were ambushed right off the bat...by an ancient Wyrm. If you're not up on relative combat strengths, the ancient

Wyrm is the boot, and my freighter the *Remora* is the bug getting squashed.

She slapped us around and ripped a hole in the hull, then threatened me specifically. The dragon wanted my Heka Aten armor, and we quickly figured out it was Headmistress Visala. The dragon I'd feared back at the Academy had turned out to be a literal Wyrm.

Anyway, my crew is pretty slippery, and my sister is one depths of a pilot. Rava crashed us into a cargo bay on the *Flame*, and I had the brilliant plan of using a sonic pulse to draw the locals to the crash site. It was my hope that they'd drive away the dragon.

They did!

Then one of these creepy scuttling arachnidrakes (who've since become friends—still creeped out... dragons and spiders should not be combined) shot me in the face with a fire bolt. You can just heal that, right? Sure, Vee took care of it with her *life* magic. But you can't regrow eyebrows. Have you ever had to pencil in eyebrows? No one takes you seriously.

Right after I lost my eyebrows I met Xal'Nara, a beautiful demon goddess, and Frit, a beautiful Ifrit goddess. Both claimed they'd come to learn more about the Vagrant Fleet, and wanted to purchase ships for their respective nations. These goddesses knew each other, and behaved a lot more like childhood friends, and less like rivals. There's a story there. I'm sure of it.

Anyway, after the hot goddess-i? goddesses? left the scene we were on our own inside a derelict and very much inhabited Great Ship. There were upsides. I found a workshop with knowledge scales dating back ten millennia. They had star charts, maps to Catalysts, and who knows what other secrets. Their value is immense, and I still have them. I just need time to study them.

We rested for the night then set out both to find something valuable enough to sell to the Confederacy, and to find parts to repair the *Remora*. Her drive was shot through, and she had a dozen other structural problems we needed to solve before she'd be even nominally space-worthy. Vee did not seem optimistic.

I figured I'd seen all the creepiness the *Flame* could throw at me, but then the Great Ship was all...hold my beer. We ran into actual spiders. Swarms of them. Every-where. Webbing in my hair. On my clothes. On my junk when I relieved myself. Gah, I crawl just thinking about it. And I'm not the one with a phobia of spiders. That's Kurz. It was bad enough that I don't want to repeat it.

These spiders arranged themselves into a face to talk to me. Turns out they belonged to something called the swarm, an insane magical intelligence created before the last godswar. What drove it mad you ask? A massively powerful artifact called the Web of Divinity.

It allows you to perceive and manipulate events across many possible realities. Past. Present. Future. What if's you've always wondered about. This thing made it all reachable.

But using it drives you insane. Remember that later.

The arachnidrake who burned off my eyebrows approached me in the ship's archive to apologize, and introduced himself as Kek. He claimed that the *Remora*'s arrival fulfilled a prophecy, and gave me a copy like a Wyrm Faithful passing out pamphlets back on Kemet.

I studied it, of course, and learned that he was right. There was a prophecy about the *Remora*. It wanted me to use a temporal matrix on the bridge, the Web of Divinity, to deposit the old *Remora*, my *Remora*, in the past, and in exchange would allow us to pull the *Remora* from 10,000 years ago into the present.

There were a few more complications before we made the attempt. An ancient and powerful Wyrm, a goddess in her own right, I'd wager, controlled much of the ship near the Web.

They were fascinated by Briff, because they don't have any *life* Wyrms on this ship. They asked him to come back with them to meet Cinaka, and he wasn't with us when we reached the bridge, which is where I accessed the Web for the first time.

The shadows still lurk in my vision, especially when I'm tired. I hear whispers sometimes, but not in any language I've ever heard. It's awesome, and by awesome, I mean terrifying.

Anyway, I accessed the temporal matrix and performed the ritual, and it worked. But I should have known every ritual has a cost. In this case the cost was my father. To bring a life to our time we had to put one back to balance the scales. My father was sucked into the past, while we brought the *Remora* and its ancient pilot into the present.

That pilot turned out to be a guy by the name of Seket, a paladin of Inura. Seket is the most handsome, dashing, honorable, tub of vanilla I have ever met. I hate him so much. But not really because infuriatingly you can't hate Seket. He's too nice. Bastard. How dare he be... awesomer than me.

During our crawl through the ship we found a forge, complete with schematics. Vee made me a pistol! Which I still haven't named. It's pretty awesome though. I'm thinking something like Eradicator. No, maybe she's Eradicata? Eh, I'll work on it.

Right around then we learned that the Inurans had begun an assault on the *Word of Xal*. They were using the legions they'd created from the survivors on Kemet, and had ordered Bortel to take the ship. That put us on a clock even more than we'd already been. Worse, the Inurans were jamming all normal and magical communication in the system preventing us from calling for help.

Kids versus hardened mercs. The kids didn't stand a chance unless I could figure out a way to bring in help.

We collected Briff from Cinaka and got ready to head back. I worried it would be a firefight, but it turned out that Cinaka and her people are massive Arena addicts. They sit around all day playing video games, and she refused to stop doing that to help us deal with Jolene and the Inurans trying to jack our fleet after blowing up our planet.

She did, however, send a platoon of her best hatchlings to help us storm the bridge and use the Web of Divinity to contact the Confederacy. I'm getting ahead of myself.

Remember me mentioning that the swarm of billions of spiders was insane? Well, it hates Cinaka and the arachnidrakes, and I'd been friendly with both groups. That meant the swarm suddenly saw me as an enemy, and the spiders decided they wanted to wipe us out.

That's where Kurz had his breakdown, but he got through it. I was impressed and proud of him for facing what he did and coming out the other side.

We clawed our way back to the bridge, and I used the Web of Divinity to break the Inuran jamming. The cost was high. I took some of the insanity into me. I can feel it. Right now. It hasn't receded or changed. It hasn't gotten worse, but it isn't getting better.

I missived a goddess named Voria, and explained the situation. If I thought my mother or the headmistress were intimidating, then this woman put them to shame. This woman could probably have them both bowing and simpering with a single glance. She scary.

Voria called in a single man. Or god, rather. A guy by the name of Crewes. Crewes brought his buddy Aran, another demon god, and proceeded to wipe the hold with Bortel's forces, saving the kids at Highspire.

I had two pretty cool pivotal bits that I added to the battle. First, we used the tobacco in Bortel's vape pen to track him, and then teleported him from commanding his forces into our brig, which denied his forces a leader during combat.

Bortel told me all about Jolene, the leader of the Inuran forces. He gave me everything I needed to assault her cruiser and deal with the woman who'd both blown up our planet and conspired to steal our legacy, the fleet itself.

Crazy as it sounds, I assembled a strike force of arachnidrakes, hatchlings, and my crew. We stormed that ship...and promptly failed. We almost reached the bridge, but were stopped by a ward that prevented teleportation.

Desperate and out of options I did what any smart adventurer does. I prayed to a demon goddess and begged for help. What could possibly go wrong?

Nara showed up and made a covenant with me. If I agreed to protect and spread knowledge, and to visit her on the Husk of Xal when I become a demigod, then she'd give me the power to survive the current situation.

I agreed. The ask didn't seem that big. If I never become a demigod, then all I have to do is protect books. I do that anyway.

I used my new weaken miracle to punch through the deck, and we stormed the bridge and wiped out the defenders. To be honest it was all a little too easy, so on a hunch I scryed the past hour until I figured out the truth.

Jolene left behind a simulacrum. A double. She got away. On the plus side? They declared her dead so she lost all her assets, including her ship. Haha. Jolene, I hope you're reading this from some seedy dive where you wipe down counters and have to wait on other people for a change.

So we won. We stopped Bortel, who is still in a cell. We kept the ship. We met our closest neighbors, the *Flame*, and helped Kek become the new ship's Guardian. If he can maintain his sanity I'm sure we'll be great friends.

And that brings us to the present. About an hour ago I got a missive from the minister to meet her on the Inuran trade moon, where our case will be heard.

If we are very lucky they'll dismiss the eleven billion credits we owe them. If not? Well, at least I'll finally be able to pass off the captaincy to my mother, and go back to being a regular relic hunter.

I can't wait.

INTERLUDE I

Necrotis wore time differently than most beings. She understood the Great Cycle itself, something that had been lost to this epoch, in this sector. Not a single god seemed aware of their origins, nor the true nature of reality and how it fueled itself.

They clung to the magic of creation, of this realm, and declared it natural. *Fire* was natural. *Life* or *air* was natural. But *void*? To be feared, because it came from elsewhere. And *spirit*? To be reviled and held in contempt, because death fueled it. *Dream* was considered nothing more than whimsy, instead of the fundamental core of the cycle that it truly was.

The sector had forgotten the artificing of necrotech, though she'd heard rumors that demotech survived among Xal's children, and that they were now making leaps forward for the first time in millennia under the guidance of some new smith. If etherealtech still existed somewhere she doubted the creators would allow word of it to escape.

All of that suited her purposes perfectly. Conquering the sector would require two things. First, she must understand her enemies. Second, she must keep them ignorant of her agenda.

She stretched both delicate hands and adjusted the heavy golden diadem until it sat perfectly along her forehead. Even now, all these millennia after she'd abandoned *life* in favor of *spirit*, long after her flesh had gone cold, she still valued appearance. And why not? Death was cold, but nothing said it could not also be beautiful.

She ascended her ivory throne, which glided into the air and hummed its way from her quarters and onto the bridge of the *Maker's Wrath*, a vessel to rival Inura's *Spellship*. All four consoles flanking the spell matrix were manned by young women with milky unseeing eyes. Silver cords connected to their temples, and better allowed them to regulate the flow of souls to the Great Ship's drive.

She'd smothered their consciousness of course. It wasn't that she feared underlings, or betrayal, or even the rise of rivals. Allowing her servants free will meant they could make mistakes. They might be a touch less agile without that will, but it meant they made unerring servants, and she valued competence over expediency.

The matrix itself held a young human man with his arms and legs lashed to the golden ring, which spun him in a slow tumbling circle. Wisps of ghostly white leaked from his chest, bits of soul slowly digested by the *Wrath*. The boy had endured three shifts, which surprised her. He would not last a fourth.

Necrotis willed her throne toward the scry-screen

dominating the far wall, which currently displayed the fleet disposition and strength of their primary opponents, the Inuran Consortium, their father's murderers and the thieves of her inheritance.

Inura had been a naive god, and had given freely. The Consortium had taken every scrap of it, including his mastery of artificing, if their ships were any indication.

Nearly three hundred capital ships were docked on the surface of the Inuran trade moon. There were no doubt countless spellfighters as well, and perhaps even a fleet of drones. Who knew what the Inurans had prepared? No one had ever assaulted a trade moon and lived to report on it, so nothing was known.

Of course, no one had ever attacked with a Great Ship, either. She could begin the assault now, if she wished, but thought better of it. Not all the pieces were in place yet.

Much had been readied. Her ship was fully restored, and the modifications they'd made to the spellcannon had been completed. Gone was the simple magitech, and in its place much more powerful necrotech. No living Inuran remembered its use.

Not even she, though Necrotis was unliving.

But Inura had kept meticulous records of his more experimental youth, and this had been his stronghold of magical creation. They'd been sealed, of course, and the wards had thwarted her for decades.

That had left her the balance of ten millennia to experiment, and thanks to the steady flow of souls from the planet Kemet she'd never lacked for subjects. She'd devoured every bit of Inura's research, and then began her own.

During that research she'd spent time in the spirit realm, something most mages didn't even realize existed. Everyone knew about the void equivalent. The Umbral Depths were critical to interstellar trade. But the ephemeral dream realm hadn't even been named by scholars, and the few who knew of the spirit realm simply called it that.

It wasn't worthy of a name like the depths, in their eyes.

That contempt was valuable, to her mind. Necrotis flourished because no one thought *spirit* powerful enough to warrant their attention. They were used to dealing with binders, such as the Krox employed. Shackling another's will horrified them, and terrified them, and made it worthy of their notice.

Animating the discarded shells of the living though? That barely warranted their attention, and they only looked at the unliving as shock troops. They had no idea how powerful, or how versatile, necrotech could be. Necrotis hadn't enjoyed much in the last several millennia. Emotions had become muted, shriveled things. This, though, she would savor.

Inura's death called out for vengeance, and the *Maker's Wrath* was finally in a position to deliver that revenge. The Consortium had grown arrogant. They believed themselves not only superior, but utterly unassailable.

How could it be that the recent godswar hadn't shaken their faith even slightly? They'd escaped unscathed. That was the reason. No one had made them pay for selling weapons to all sides, and for ultimately unleashing a dark goddess on the sector.

All of it had been laid at the feet of one man. A scape-goat they'd conjured named Skare, possibly the ugliest Inuran she'd seen in all her years of unlife. The Inurans had martyred one of their own, and in exchange been afforded total clemency.

Just as they'd gone unpunished for betraying the Vagrant Fleet, all those millennia ago. Necrotis closed her eyes, and suppressed the childish impulse to reach for her old name. To be the woman she'd been in life, the dutiful Outrider, and highly decorated officer on Inura's own vessel.

No, she'd abandoned that when she'd murdered this ship, then raised its soul as a weapon capable of ending the Inurans forever. And that was only the beginning.

She offered a cruel smile to the uncaring scry-screen. She could see them, but they labored in ignorance. None of her enemies had the slightest inkling of her existence.

The sector had no idea what they were in store for. They'd spent the better part of a decade knocking each other down as hard as possible. Entire Catalysts had been devoured. Gods had appeared, and had just as predictably been killed.

Enough had survived to form a pantheon, though, and that was new and troubling enough to stir her to action. She didn't fear any single one of these new "gods", but that didn't mean she wasn't wary. She, too, possessed divinity. She was no pathetic mortal necromancer.

She was a goddess, a dark, terrible, vengeful goddess. Inura's barren daughter.

Her smile increased when the last fly entered the web, the cruiser designated *Remora* gliding down into the trade moon's artificial atmosphere. The minister of the few surviving Kemetian sheep had already arrived, and the captain of the *Word of Xal* was about to. That last gave her pause. This Jerek had been aboard the *Flame of Knowledge*, if her spies were accurate. Had he touched the Web? What had he learned there? Was he aware of her or her plans?

The *Word of Xal* had been engineered by Inura and Xal together, and in some ways might eclipse her own vessel. She seriously doubted they had the magic to fight a prolonged engagement, but she hadn't survived this long without being prudent. That ship could hurt her. Perhaps destroy the *Wrath* itself. That made this captain dangerous.

Still, the rewards were great. If she won an engagement, then she could add the *Word* to her fleet. Once she finished outfitting it with necrotech there wasn't a force in the sector who would voluntarily enter an engagement with her.

Then, in a few short years, she'd reactivate the trade moon and the rest of the ships, and retrofit them with her discoveries. She would take the sector, and if no one stopped her...the galaxy.

It had begun as a quest for vengeance, and it was that still, but she'd lived long enough to think very carefully about what came after the extermination of the Inuran Consortium.

All roads led to victory. She'd made certain of it. And when victory was certain you had plenty of time to dwell on the after.

For now she needed to act. The next few hours would secure the first phase of her plan.

Everything on that trade moon was about to die screaming.

1

The bullshit began the moment I stepped off the *Remora*'s landing pad, and into the Inuran welcome chamber. A high ceiling with a glass roof provided an epic view of the Vagrant Fleet, though the graffiti on the walls of the atrium's lower level said this place wasn't as fancy as the designers had hoped it would be.

I hadn't wanted to come to the trade moon at all, but my mother had insisted this was where the transfer of power would take place. This was where I'd turn over the captaincy I'd worked so hard to attain.

I fully agreed with her logic, and didn't want to run the *Word of Xal* myself, but it was still like a toy being taken away. Yeah, I was petulant about it. I owned it. I'd chosen to go by myself, because my crew disagreed with my choice. They wanted me to keep the captaincy.

A crowd awaited me at the bottom of the ramp, with the immaculately dressed minister at the center of her retinue. Behind and back a few paces lurked the security detail, and closer stood the various attendants jockeying for power. I recognized my mother, who wore Heka Aten armor, like mine, with the helmet retracted. No smile. Damn. She was here on business.

The minister gave me turbo lift eyes, and took no pains to hide her annoyance, which of course triggered mine. She wasn't the one being ambushed.

"Hello, Minister," I managed as cheerfully as three hours sleep would allow. I'd just returned from dropping off Cinaka and her surviving hatchings on the *Flame*, and now I badly wanted sleep. "I wasn't expecting you or your, uh, friends until morning. You offered us a stay at that fancy hotel, remember? My crew have been tolerant, but the cracks are showing. They need rest."

"I realize that, and I sympathize. Nevertheless, we're getting this over with. Now." Minister Ramachan plucked at the sleeve of her jacket, then smoothed the blouse. "This place unmakes me. The Inurans have spies everywhere. In fact, I'm shocked their personal shopping assistants haven't glommed onto us yet. They flock like carrion cleaners. This is our last moment of privacy, Jerek, and I wanted to do this with as much dignity as possible. Please. Don't make this difficult. You've already agreed."

I licked my lips, and wished I had another hour to think, even though I knew it wouldn't help me in the slightest. Impossible situations couldn't be solved with more time.

"Of course, but first I want a moment alone with my mother." I fixed my mom with my best captain's stare, which had improved a lot after surviving both the *Flame of Knowledge* and the raid on Jolene's ship. It still wasn't easy. "We need to talk, Irala."

That was the first time I'd ever uttered my mother's first name when addressing her, and it hung between us.

"All right." My mother licked her lips, and nodded at a corner of the room. She'd begun sketching brilliant grey and blue sigils even before I joined her, far more rapidly than I'd ever be able to manage, and quickly assembled a privacy ward that rippled outward to surround us both. Once it had completed she nodded at me. "Say what you need to, but please don't try to wriggle out of this."

"If you have a shred of respect for me you'll treat this with the gravity it deserves." I folded my arms to mirror her judge-y stance, and forced myself to look her in the eye. "This isn't about me trying to hold onto power. This is about you misusing it once you have it." My tone rose, and the words came faster. "I can't say I'm overly fond of your girlfriend, Mom. She cut and ran. Visala can be ruthless, but she wasn't wrong about the minister. Staying could have made a difference. I saw the numbers. It was touch and go until I brought in the Confederacy. And, not to be a little brat, but it *was* me that brought them in. I have a vested interest in this. I don't want to turn the ship over to you only to watch helplessly as the minister aims it at her next problem."

My mother stood before the tide of my anger, an immovable, weathered rock of parental stoicism. "Are you done, or was there more?"

"There's a lot more." I lowered my hands, which had begun to shake. "Mom, that ship can destroy continents once fully powered. Maybe a planet. You overcame the trials right? Are we allowed to talk about them now that we're both officers?"

Mom opened her mouth, then after a moment of frustration, closed it again. She barked a brittle laugh. "Not directly, it seems. Well I know what I saw, and I'll assume it was the same for you. The ship made me face hard choices, and solve difficult puzzles. I'm impressed you overcame the second one. It's been a long time since you were interested in Kem'Hedj."

That last was more than I'd expected the geas to allow. A spell like that was woven into our very soul, and had specific dictates. I needed to better understand the limitations. I wanted to know what had been done to me, especially after spending time on the *Flame*. The shadows still lurked in the corners, and while there were no more of them...there were never any less, either.

"It sounds like we witnessed the same trials. I found the last the most challenging, but the first one shook me." I shuddered as I remembered tumbling silently through the darkness with no idea if or how fast I was moving, or where I was falling to. "Mom, there is one more thing. This ship is more important than the other Great Ships. The Guardian, Kemet...you know who he was?"

She eyed me in that exasperated way she'd always had whenever something had taken me longer than it should to grasp. My mother had taught me to be a scholar, because she loved knowledge too. I wasn't surprised she knew of him.

Mom glanced through the ward at the minister. "He was the admiral of the fleet that brought us here, and that made this the flagship. How ironic that our culture has forgotten him almost entirely. It stands to reason that the most important secrets or artifacts are likely stored on the *Word*. I was a relic hunter too, for a time. What are you hiding?"

"If Kemet hasn't told you then I'm not sure I can." I'd been about to say should. If she accepted the lie, or rejected it, I couldn't tell.

"So there is something important linked to the ship. Maybe he'll tell me after you promote me." She reached up and scrubbed both hands through thick rivers of dark hair, then paused for a steep yawn. "Jerek, honey, I want to assure you. I am my own person, not a mouthpiece. Not even for her. And yes, I do love her and trust her, but if she asked me to do something against my principles I would refuse. I am not a mass murderer. I was against fleeing when the assault on the *Word* began, but the minister's cabinet voted almost unanimously to go. Some of us surviving was better than none. It was the wrong call, but that's only clear with hindsight. At the time...I made a mistake."

That shocked me. I'd seen my mother wrong exactly twice in my life. Both had been minor mathematical errors, swiftly rectified.

"I'm the very last person in the sector who'll judge you for that, Mom. You, ah, didn't ask about Dad. I have news. He went out how he wanted." I raised my hand and extended it palm outwards, and I didn't bother to hide the tears. "Once you're captain you can speak to Kemet about his secret. If he chooses to share it, that's up to him."

"I'm glad your father had a chance to find himself again. I wish I could have—you've studied the procedure?" My mother raised her hand, and pressed it against mine, then gave me a squeeze. The Heka Aten armor was an amazing feat of engineering, and transferred the touch perfectly.

"Of course I've studied it." I tried on a tentative smile, in spite of the shards of glass in my belly that dad's death had left. "Have you met my mother? I always read the manual first. The process is simple, and mostly verbal. We'll need Guardian as witness, which means we'll need our masks on."

I wondered how far Guardian would be able to transmit if the core were fully powered? We were half a system away, but he'd reached further when I'd been on Kemet.

My helmet slithered over my face, and by the time the HUD lit and began populating with data my mom had also donned her helmet. Neither one of us liked expressing emotion, and that had been...a lot.

"Guardian," I intoned into my comm. "This is acting Captain Jerek of the *Word of Xal*. I hereby invoke the right of transfer, and cede my rank and title to Irala, who stands before me."

A surge of frigid current raced from my heart, through my arm, and into my palm. The magic burst from my hand, and had my fingers not been interlocked with my mother's, our hands would have burst apart from the force of it.

The magic disappeared into her gauntlet, and she fell

back with a gasp. Mom straightened and raised a hand, almost instantly. "I'm fine. I just need a moment."

"I can't believe it was that fast. I guess they designed the process for combat situations."

Once I was certain she was okay I probed within myself. The *void* magic was still there. The connection to the *Word* was still there. I couldn't tell what it was exactly I'd lost, though I could feel the difference, like a missing tooth.

A scarlet notification appeared on the HUD, and I willed it to the forefront. A holographic representation of the Inuran trade moon and the *Word of Xal* appeared in my field of view.

A third object appeared, roughly the same size as the *Word*, and much smaller than the trade moon. Another Great Ship?

"What am I looking at, Guardian?"

"I believe," Guardian began as a holographic dragon hatchling appeared beneath the ships, "that we are looking at the *Inura's Grace*. I do not know who flies her, or what their intentions, but they approach swiftly."

2

I f you guessed that I had absolutely no time to process an approaching Great Ship, you'd be right. My mother immediately dropped the ward, and rushed over to the minister's side, her helmet still up.

"Minister, you're aware of the approaching threat?" She glanced up and over her shoulder, and when I followed that gaze I saw it land on the holographic ships. Guess our HUDs were linked.

"Is it done?" The minister's eyes tightened as she faced my mother. "Are you in control of that ship?"

"I am." My mother placed a hand on the minister's shoulder. "Div, we need to go. Now."

"You're not making sense. Explain." The minister raised a hand and patted her bun as if inspecting for loose hairs.

"There is an approaching Great Ship, and we have no idea of its intent." My mother nodded up the corridor, presumably the way from which they'd come. "We can be back to our ship in five minutes. We have control over the

Word. We can't jeopardize that. A ship needs a captain, especially if there's the possibility of battle."

The minister nodded, but took a step backward and massaged her temples. "I'm thinking. Just give me a moment." She was silent for a good thirty seconds, then opened her eyes and rammed some steel into her posture. "Irala, you are to take the *Spear of Seket* back to the *Word*. Get on top of the situation, and keep me updated. We cannot afford to flee, however, until we know that ship is a threat. If we can't ink a deal today we may not get another chance, and our survival hangs in the balance. We don't just need their cooperation. We need the supplies they can sell us."

"I understand." My mother embraced the minister, which earned some shocked gasps from attendants. "Be careful." Then she turned to me. "Jerek, I need your help. If she's staying she needs protection. Can you take your crew and get her to her meeting, then bring her straight back to the *Word* the moment it's over?"

"I'll get it done, Captain." And I meant it. "Minister, I need ten minutes to assemble my crew and get geared up."

"You don't have it." The minister turned and began walking back the way she'd come, her entire retinue in tow. She paused a dozen steps in, and faced me. "I'll have the coordinates of the meeting sent, and let the Inurans know to expect you. The meeting will be brief, and I will use your ship to return to the *Spear of Seket*. Please keep your engines hot, if that applies to spelldrives."

Then she was off again, and I didn't try to follow. I needed to get my people up, and fast. This wasn't the kind of mission we were trained or equipped for, but I had been asked to do more with less. My mom needed this done, and whether I liked the minister or not she wasn't just an important part of our government. She was extended family.

I darted back up the ramp and into the *Remora*'s aft cargo hold. Briff and Rava were both awake, and both drinking, while playing an entirely too loud game of Arena. It wasn't nearly as bad as when Cinaka and her hatchlings were aboard, but it still made thinking difficult.

I didn't want to draft either into service. They could stay here with the ship. So who did I take? Kurz was the most respectable, but he was badly shaken by his time aboard the *Flame*, even more than I had been. He needed time to process and decompress.

That left Vee and Seket. I should leave Seket here as he was our only qualified pilot, but if I needed to safe-guard the minister then I needed our best fighter with me.

I trotted to the mess, and as expected found Vee busily scanning a tablet as she worked on a holo of a grenade. It took everything to suppress the sudden urge to pepper her with questions about what she was design-ing, but seconds counted.

"Hey, we've got trouble," I called, loudly enough to get her attention. Vee glanced up with a smile, but it faded when she caught my expression. "The minister needs us to escort her back from a meeting, and we need to get there now. I figured you'd be able to counter any BS their artificers try. Can you be ready in two?"

"Who else is coming?" She rose with a stretch and a cavernous yawn. "And what aren't you telling me?"

I'd hoped to avoid this part until we were underway, but I knew she wouldn't budge without at least a little more info. "The *Inura's Grace* is on approach. I don't know what your connection to that ship is, but you might want to think about sharing. I'd love to know who's flying her, and whether or not I can expect an attack. We're going to have to discuss it on the run, though. I need to find Seket."

"But...that...." She trailed off as she swayed toward the doorway, hobbled by what I'd just told her. "That shouldn't be possible. We were told we're centuries from repairing the ship's drive. No one is allowed aboard, so we couldn't verify, but...have they been lying to us?" She shook her head, then looked up at me. "I can't tell you everything just now. There's too much to think about. I'll meet you at the aft airlock."

I nodded. It was enough. Then I turned from the mess and headed up to the bridge, which was where I'd find Seket. As expected, Seket stood in the spell matrix, in full spellarmor, despite the ship being at rest.

"Do you sleep in there?" I asked. "Or do you just not require sleep?"

"I do sleep." Seket turned to face me, his golden helmet clutched loosely under one arm. "But it is standard operating procedure to have two pilots on deck at all times. As we only have two pilots if you are away from the ship, then my place is here. Find another pilot, and I will take my ease."

"You're going to hate this ask then." I still had my

helmet up, but I'm sure he could detect the weariness in my voice. "We need to guard the minister's person. She's at a meeting, and we have been tasked with getting her back from it safely, and then taking her to her flagship. I'd like you to personally tend to her safety, until we get back to the *Remora* and can install you on the bridge."

"And if the *Remora* is attacked while we are gone?" He raised a perfect blond eyebrow. "I do not like leaving her without a pilot. She is grounded. Vulnerable."

"Rava has *fire* magic now, and is a quick study. She can pilot in an emergency." I turned before he could respond, since I couldn't counter any of his objections. Rava would be a terrible pilot, until she was trained at least. She'd never worked with magic, and had no idea how to operate a spell matrix. "We need to move. We're already behind, in an unfamiliar place. I'll meet you at the aft airlock."

Seket didn't reply, but a moment later I heard the clanking of his booted feet on the deck as he followed. I used the short walk to the airlock to try to find my footing, but was instead distracted by random thoughts.

Why didn't the trade moon have atmosphere? Why not cover the surface with forests to sustain oxygen? Another ship lifted off in the distance. Oh. Atmo created drag, and would be terrible for shipping.

I arrived at the airlock and found Vee waiting in an unfamiliar blue uniform with gold trim. There might have been patches on the shoulder, but it looked as if they'd been skillfully removed.

"I found it in my quarters," Vee answered my unasked question with a blush. "I figured it was more...formal than my clothes. I don't want them to assume I'm some sort of yokel. I'm every bit as good at artificing as they are. They just keep a stranglehold on the market, and call themselves the best while quietly smothering competition."

Seket clanked his way up behind us, then snapped his left wrist down and ignited a blue-white spellshield. He made no move to draw a weapon. "I am prepared. I will fight defensively if we're engaged, unless you designate a target, Captain."

"Thanks, Sek." I turned back to the ramp that led back to the welcome chamber where I'd met the minister. "Let's be quick about this. I want to get there before the *Inura's Grace* does whatever it's going to do.

"You think it might attack this moon?" The question held no contempt, though it sounded ludicrous when he said it out loud. He seemed to be seeking tactical data, and it took a moment for me to remember that he came from a time when planets were routinely blown up by gods.

He already knew this place wasn't safe, a notion that had just taken root with me. What if the ship was strong enough to attack the moon? Or the *Word*? Either was bad for people I cared about.

"We're not going to be here long enough to find out. In and out. Let's go."

3

We raced down the ramp, and I'll be honest, we looked kind of badass. I took the lead with my still unnamed pistol belted at my thigh, and Vee to my right, with Seket trailing behind both of us.

I glanced up through an enormous atrium window at the glittering Vagrant Fleet high in orbit, and realized I could easily make out the *Inura's Grace*. Too easily. It appeared much larger than the *Word*, now. That thing was headed our way.

I redoubled my speed and we raced down the atrium walkway, toward the corridor at the far side on the lower level. We'd made it maybe 50 meters when a gorgeous woman with dark hair and alabaster skin fell into step next to me. It was like meeting Seket's just as hot cousin.

"A moment of your time," she panted, while managing to keep pace with our sprint. "My name is Miri and your minister thought you could use help getting to the arbitration."

"The minister sent you?" I panted back. Physical exertion was easier for me in the sense that it was now possible, but even with the armor I didn't enjoy running. "What's the fastest way to the meeting?"

So why suddenly trust a stranger? Because thanks to my connection to the Web of Divinity no one could lie to me. She had to be telling the truth, or I'd know.

"If you'll follow me." She sprinted past me and took the lead. Easily. This woman was a lifelong athlete of the type who could have competed in our Lympic games.

I took a guilty moment to enjoy watching her run, which was impossible not to do with her white uniform painted onto those legs. I noted the spellpistol belted on one thigh, and eventually, many moments later, my eyes made it past her ass and up to her back.

There was a logo emblazoned on her uniform. A smiling Inuran in a white uniform pushing a cart full of guns.

"Who do you work for?" I called after her. Speaking triggered a stitch in my side, but I stubbornly redoubled my pace. Every time I wanted to slow I heard my father's voice.

I knew exactly what he'd say. *Son, I died for you. And now you gotta feel guilty. Keep working out. Or I'll haunt you.* Depths but I missed him.

I strained for a bit more speed, and while I couldn't keep up with FTL up there at least I didn't fall behind Vee or Seket. We ran for perhaps three hundred more meters through twisting corridors, and up several flights of stairs.

We emerged into what I took to be a basement, prob-

ably of a large structure. I could hear thunderous
applause inside, though it ended quickly.

Miri skidded to a halt before the doors, and if she was
winded I couldn't tell. She withdrew a Quantum-enabled
tablet from a large pocket in her jacket. "I'll make this
quick as I know you're in a hurry. I'm your personal shopping assistant. We're sometimes called solicitors, if people
are being nice, or things like spam, ad puppet, or glom if
we're not. I'd prefer either PSA or Miri, but you're the
client, so you decide."

"Let's go with Miri. And you help me do what, exactly?" I knew I needed to get inside, but found myself fascinated by whatever her job was. Why did I need a PSA
with a gun?

"I'm glad you asked." Her smile embarrassed the best
sunset ever, though it contained an artificial note. "You're
here to acquire something. In this case, the minister.
When you complete this task you'll pay me a nominal
fee, plus a gratuity if you feel my service warrants it."

I nodded along. This was amazing. "And in this
service there might be cause for you to shoot someone?"

"Of course." She blinked me as if the question made
no sense. "Are you unfamiliar with the regulations? That
sign indicates that we're in a black area. You are responsible for your own security, though if you report a crime it
will be logged, and then ignored, unless you have enough
credits to pay for their attention. It's my job to keep you
alive, and if I can't, well...let's just say I'm not some helpless mechanic."

The last two words left her mouth like missiles and
streaked into Vee, who'd just skidded up behind me.

Seket lumbered up a moment later, just in time to miss the biting comment. The timing was too precise to be coincidence, though Miri's tone was still sweet as pie.

"Did you just call me helpless?" Vee's eyes fixed on our new PSA. "And you work in a tip based profession? How does that work, exactly?"

Miri blinked at Vee as if she were being unreasonable, but the shopping assistant were magnanimously over-looking it. How she communicated that with an expression I don't know, but convey it she did. "I didn't mean you, miss. Please. I would never offer offense to a client. Though, to be fair, you are not my client and will not be paying any tip I might receive."

"Uh huh." Vee frowned at her, but looked away.

"Where to now? In there?" I nodded at the chamber where the clapping emanated from.

She laughed prettily and shook her head.

"That's the council chamber, but your matter is far too trivial to be heard there. We're taking a lift down to level 36, in arbitration chamber J-6."

She turned and trotted toward an unobtrusive pair of grey doors set into the wall. We were already starting in the basement, but we needed to go down thirty-six levels? The idea that our planet's dissolution warranted nothing more than a side room boiled my blood, but I knew expressing that anger would only delay me leaving this wretched place.

"There's good news," Miri offered as she pressed the down arrow set into the wall next to the lift door. "We're entering an orange area. Automated security has been installed, which discourages most open violence.

Snipers and the occasional explosive still get used, but that's rare unless someone is acting on a grudge. Destroying a turret will get you hunted down, and no one wants that."

I don't know what I'd expected, but thus far the trade moon was anything but that. I'd thought the Inurans must be the most orderly, restrictive lot in the sector, but the surface of their moon was a lawless wasteland where anyone could have their gear jacked? How did that make for repeat business?

The answer was right there. Where else were you going to go? If you couldn't afford your own security, then you weren't wealthy enough to matter.

The lift doors opened with a reluctant sigh, and Miri drew her pistol, then advanced inside. "Clear! Get in. Quickly."

I drew my pistol as I entered the urine-soaked lift, and noted that Vee's bracelet had begun to glow. We were as ready as we could be. I scanned the button panel, and stabbed 36. The buttons went all the way down to 99, and below that there was a fatter button that read *Reactor*. I didn't ask.

The lift whirred into motion, and we began to descend at an alarming rate, far faster than any lift I'd ever been aboard back on Kemet. I seized the bar running at about waist height, which wasn't too dissimilar from a matrix's stabilizing ring.

Twenty queasy seconds later the lift hummed to a halt, and the doors protested mightily as they slid open. The level stretching before us was dimly lit, and many of the lumifixtures had failed entirely. Refuse receptacles dotted the main chamber outside the lifts, and every one overflowed with garbage.

Dozens of workers in drab grey or white uniforms scurried to and from the lifts, though not a one darted a furtive glance our way. It reminded me of where I'd grown up. Pretending like you don't see became an ingrained defense mechanism. They were praying we'd ignore them.

"This way." Miri wrapped a hand around my forearm and squeezed gently. "Follow me."

She hurried into the crowd, which parted before her as if they knew who, or what, she was. I didn't know the cultural significance of these PSAs, but if they were incredible athletes and mages, and also well armed, then it stood to reason people probably feared them.

There were a few others with similar uniforms who seemed to be scanning the crowd. One, a short wiry man even started toward me with a sales pitch.

I ignored him and trotted after Miri, who passed a row of holoscreens, all displaying the same reporter, a woman who could have been Miri's sister, though with platinum hair and darker skin. I couldn't hear whatever she was chatting merrily about, but I saw the *Inura's Grace* displayed behind her. The Great Ship chilled me the core, though I couldn't say why. The reporter certainly didn't seem alarmed.

Miri skidded to a halt outside a pair of bleak metal doors. She withdrew a keycard, inserted it, then uttered an incantation under her breath. The doors popped open with a thunk, and she slipped inside, then beckoned me to follow. "Keep silent, and sit in the back row."

I recognized the stench the moment I entered. It was a unique blend of poorly circulated atmo, fermenting garbage left too long in bins, and of course the stink of human fear. It was a court after all.

The room didn't seem too different than a Kemetian courtroom had been. Six rows of uncomfortable metal chairs were bisected by a walkway that led from the door to the ancient basalt throne where the judge lounged. Real ancient Terran stuff. I bet the stone was as fake as the justice you received.

Nearly every seat was occupied. Over half those attending were drifters, most clutching a wad of paperwork in one hand and a beer in the other.

The remainder were human, with only a few shabbily dressed Inurans thrown in. It seemed pretty clear why this specific courtroom had been chosen for our arbitration.

I scanned the crowd until I found the minister, but unfortunately it appeared the case had already begun. A regal man with hawkish eyebrows and long silver hair sat atop the throne. He was handsome, in an Inuran way, but not the Seket level of handsome. He studied the proceedings carefully, then inclined his head to the group of Inurans sitting at the table opposite the minister.

"I, Lord Aruni, have been designated judge and executioner over all cases heard in this courtroom today." He leaned forward in his chair. "I do not tire. I will not grow bored. However, I may become irritated. Do not irritate me. Who speaks for the Inuran Consortium?"

"I do, your excellence." A young Inuran with platinum hair rose to his feet. "I am sub-assistant Sarkor, of the Inuran Consortium. I have come to defend our interests. If it pleases the court, may I present the case we'd like arbitrated?"

"Go on." Judge Aruni flung a leg over the arm of his throne, and adopted an expression that belied his earlier claim about getting bored.

Sarkor rose to his feet and approached the throne. "A now deceased member of the Inuran Consortium, Matron Jolene, caused the destruction of the planet Kemet. Just prior to this she signed a legally binding contract to have a trade moon brought to this system. While we are most regretful that her crimes cannot be punished, we adhered to our part of the arrangement. The trade moon is here. If there is no commerce, then barring some catastrophic emergency that forces us to depart the system the cancellation fee is still owed. That is what we are here to discuss."

"So if I understand your case," Aruni drawled as he studied the fingernails on one hand, "one of our Matrons destroyed a planet, and you believe that we should extort the surviving refugees of wealth they do not possess."

"Precisely." Sarkor relaxed and offered a friendly smile. "Their loss is tragic, and we understand that the refugees may not have the entirety of the credits. We'd be willing to settle for their claim on the balance of the Vagrant Fleet. They keep the—"

A klaxon eradicated all sound. The man's mouth was moving, for a moment anyway, but I heard nothing. No one did. Every last person had their hands cupped over their ears, and the situation was worsened by a strobing light at the top of the room.

An automated voice rang from speakers set into the wall. "An emergency has occurred. Please make your way to the surface in an orderly fashion. You are responsible for your own safety. However, if you wish we have many personal shopping assistants available to alleviate your security concerns."

I realized I was still standing in the aisle. I ordered my mask to slither over my face to escape the ear-shattering siren, and gave a relieved sigh when my HUD lit. The pain receded immediately, though I could still hear the muffled pandemonium.

"Guardian, get me a holo up that includes my current location, relative to the *Inura's Grace*." I forced a calming breath as the klaxon continued. The holo with the Vagrant Fleet and the Inuran trade moon returned.

A pallid glow began to build in the Great Ship's enormous spellcannon, and then discharged. Mute horror robbed me of all reason as that terrible writhing beam slammed into the trade moon, right on top of our current location.

Were they shooting directly at me?

4

The entire courtroom shook, and those not already sitting were dashed to the floor or into the metal chairs. Blackness smothered the chaos, for a moment anyway, as the power failed.

Then it snapped back on, and exposed dozens of confused people climbing to their feet. Almost all clutched bleeding wounds from where they'd struck metal or stone.

At least the klaxon had stopped.

Miri shook her head and had an unfocused look to her gaze, but seemed to be recovering.

"Guardian, what kind of weapon just hit the trade moon?" I demanded as I drew my pistol. "Why are we still alive? It was right on top of us."

I wasn't the only one prepared to defend myself. Weapons were coming out all over the room. Definitely not the kind of courtroom I was used to, though I noticed that not a single person fired. Hadn't Miri said something about turrets?

"The beam contained tens of thousands of spirits," the Guardian's voice echoed over my internal comm, even as the holo updated to display a tide of grey dots engulfing the entire surface of the moon. "I suspect the majority are wights, but there were more powerful souls toward the center of the beam. I would advise caution. This assault will quickly become global, and their numbers will only grow. You are at the very center of the blast."

"How close to the center? Am I being paranoid? It can't be a coincidence that they targeted our location." I loved how understated he could be about things. "I don't need an answer. I know that isn't important right now. We need to focus on getting back to the *Remora*. I've seen wights in action. I can't imagine that many, especially with there being no defenses on the surface."

Miri began shouldering her way through the crowd toward the minister, while the rest of the people stampeded the opposite direction through the doors and towards the lift.

I followed and took advantage of the wake she'd created. People definitely got out of her way, though I still had no idea if that was her rank, or more likely, her reputation.

I came up short next to the minister, and noted that the hawk-eyed judge and prosecutor had both moved to join her. The three were conferring in low tones, and I caught the tail end of their conversation as I approached.

"...All going to die," Sarkor growled, then stalked toward the lift. I don't think I even registered in his vision as I walked past him, toward the minister. "I'm taking my people and getting out of here."

"Running for that lift is suicide," the minister snapped. She nodded at me as I joined her, but didn't stop her speech. "We need to get back to the surface. I have a ship waiting. You're welcome to accompany us, Sarkor. Even if you are an asshole."

The sub-assistant halted at that. "I'll be going my own way, once we reach the lift. I need to get down to the reactor. There's an express lift from there that will get me to my ship. The rest of you lot can die for all I care. Most of you already have."

I stepped between the Inuran and the minister. We didn't have time for this.

"Are you ready to be escorted to my ship?" I asked. I didn't really care about the rest of it. Vee and Seket stood behind me, and I was responsible for their safety and the minister's.

"My aides are screaming that the surface is crawling with spirits, and that they've had to lift off. We have nothing on the surface that isn't being overrun." She shivered at that, and dropped eye contact. "I can't abide spirits. They're unnatural."

Vee cleared her throat, and took a step closer to join the conversation. "On that we can most definitely agree. They're unnatural. The maker's scriptures are quite clear, and I've seen what such spirits can do. We need to go. Now."

"I'm not sure I agree," I said, thinking aloud. That earned me some fun looks from everyone, especially Sarkor. "Hear me out. We do need to reach the surface, but coming out anywhere near the lift we came in on is asking to get overwhelmed by wights, or maybe worse. Is there another way up? Something far from an occupied area? If we can find a shaft up to the surface then the *Remora* can come pick us up."

"You can't be serious." Seket delivered a scandalized frown. "Rava isn't trained. If she crashes that ship we're all dead. Be smart, Captain. It's a walk, to be sure, but let's get there on foot. I'd suggest telling them to stay put and prepare for spirits. If you have salt...use it."

"We have a forge," I pointed out. I thumbed the comm. "Briff are you reading me?"

"Yeah, Jer," the dragon's frightened voice came back over the com. "Kurz says we'll be okay if we stay in the mess. Or on the bridge. He put down these lines of salt. Will that really work?"

"It'll work." I closed my eyes for a moment. "Buddy, you're going to have to take charge, and you might need to help Rava fly the ship. We're going to work our way back to you, but if you are getting overwhelmed, then you're going to have to convince Rava to take off. Or you're going to have to do it. Those are her options."

I knew that would give my sister the courage. There was no way she'd let Briff try to pilot anything. But it didn't mean she'd be competent at it.

Seket ground his teeth audibly, but at least the paladin didn't question the order, though I knew he strongly disagreed with it.

"Minister, I—"

"I'm going with you." Judge Aruni took a step closer and loomed over me like a parent scolding a toddler.

Damn, they made these people tall. "You are Captain Jerek, yes?"

"Uh." I licked my lips and was glad he couldn't see my face through the mask. "I find it kind of alarming that you know who I am."

"Your name is mentioned frequently in the case files I perused." Aruni folded his arms and nodded at the slowly shrinking crowd forcing itself through the doors and into the already overpacked corridors. "Once that lot has thinned out I'd like an escort to the surface. I can pay."

I blinked at that. This wasn't about money. It was about survival. I wasn't stupid though. "What are you offering?"

"I want to look you in the eye if we're to make a deal," Aruni waved a hand, and my HUD went dark, then the helmet slithered off my face. "I am offering justice. I will rule in your favor. The debt will be forgiven."

Miri choked and by the time I glanced in her direction her mouth had begun working like some poor sucker that had just been spaced. "They'll...you'll be ruined. Your career is over."

"This moon is over," Aruni countered with a raised eyebrow, thrust like a spellblade. "I understand what's coming. Every citizen unable to defend themselves will rise as a wight. Or worse. When they turn they will turn others. The spread is...well, you've seen nothing in the life of your world that will prepare you for what is about to happen. I wish to live. Get me to the surface, Captain. I am not blind. I see the paladin and the lurker girl in her moth-eaten uniform. You have the tools to get me to the surface. I have the tools to save your people officially."

"Done." I didn't even need to think about it. I turned to the minister. "I haven't tried to reach Mom yet. I don't know how these hostiles are going to deal with the *Word*, but we have to assume they'll have an aggressive plan. If you deal with that situation, then I'll get us back to the ship."

"I don't like it. I don't like any of it," she groused, but she was already nodding. "Get us to the surface, and to your ship, or another one that will get us away from this cursed place." She spared a glance for Aruni. "I don't trust him to follow through on his promise, but I suppose there's no harm in keeping him alive. Maybe he'll soak up a spell, or slow down a wight long enough for someone who matters to get away."

Aruni began to laugh, the kind of joyous laugh of someone pleasantly delighted to have learned something. "You are a true joy, Minister. I will follow through. I will follow through and more, I assure you."

"Seket?" I asked into the squad comm.

"Yes, Captain?" His tone transmitted every grievance, though his helmet was on and I didn't have to endure the smugness directly.

"Find us a route to a stairwell," I ordered.

Vee's voice whispered onto the comm. "Won't the stairwell be packed with people fleeing when they realize the lifts are full?"

"Yes, but we won't be going up." I closed my eyes and thought back to the lift. "There's a reactor down there. A reactor is big, and probably doesn't require a large staff.

We skirt the reactor and move laterally until we're directly under the *Remora*, or as close as we can be, and then we look for lift."

"It's workable," Seket allowed. He began clanking his way to the back of the line. A deep, booming voice issued from his armor. "Step aside! Now! Judge Aruni is passing through."

The crowd somehow melted before us, enough that we were able to force a path. I held on tightly to the minister, and was conscious of Vee behind me. She looked innocent enough with that ponytail, but I'd been shot by her and knew how quick she was on the draw.

The crowd thinned as we bypassed the lifts and made for a pair of doors marked with an icon of a stairwell.

Frantic screams came from within.

5

I didn't think. I acted. Sometimes that is a really bad idea. Sometimes, though, acting can save some-one's life.

I blinked through the door and into pandemonium. A few stray beams from headlamps were the only illumina-tion, save for a ghostly glow that flowed down the stair-well above us in an inevitable tide of hungry death.

"Downstairs as fast as you can. Go, go!" I yelled, even as I realized who I was yelling at. A team of pristine Inuran mages in scout spellarmor had been about to try the door to our level. I counted six, but in the darkness it was hard to be certain. "Get to a fortified position down there. If you have *life* mages or salt, set up a barrier. We're going to be dealing with a whole lot of wights."

"Yes, sir," a feminine voice issued from the armor closest to me as she snapped a fist over her heart. "We'll fortify the next level. Who are you escorting?"

Of course she assumed I was someone's bodyguard. I planted my foot against the door and channeled an infuse strength spell, then kicked as hard as I could. Nothing.

Then I remembered. I had miracles from Xal'Nara. I rested a hand against the door's magi-scanner and whispered, "Weaken."

Rust rippled outward from where I'd touched, and the entire panel flaked away. I kicked the door again, and it flung inward in a shower of rust as the last of it dissolved.

"Down. Quickly!"

I guided Judge Aruni through, and as I did so the buzzing in the back of my head rose to an urgent pitch. There was something about him. Something my gift from the *Flame of Knowledge* should allow me to see. Then the buzzing faded, and Aruni was past me.

I helped the minister through next, then Sarkor's still sneering face afterwards. When Seket entered I nodded at the stairwell. "Hey, can you get your aura up? We need to keep them at bay long enough to fortify a defensive position, or this is going to end badly."

"Yes, Captain." Seket stepped forward, and his entire armor flared a brilliant white-gold. He extended a hand and his void pocket opened, a vertical slash in reality I wished I could crawl into. Out came his spellblade, which also flared in brilliant challenge.

The tide of wights finally rounded the last bend onto the stairwell above our level, and their layered shrieks grew into a frustrated frenzy when they realized they could come no closer.

"Nice work." I capped Seket on the back, then turned to Vee, who'd been lurking in the doorway. "Get down there and back the Inurans up. Be ready to use your aura, but only if we have to. I want to save that until later, if we can. You can only do that once a day, right?"

"Yeah." She bit her lip. Then shook her head. "I'll try hard not to have to use it. They might have salt down there, or a forge so I can make more."

Then she was trotting down the steps, her ponytail bobbing behind her. She had her helmet cupped around her free hand opposite the bracelet, and I realized she was using it as an improvised shield. Smart. Her armor wouldn't stop spirits, so no sense having it on for wights.

A stream of people from the courtroom flowed down the stairs after her. I recognized a drifter I'd seen, and a hatchling with a black patch of scales over half his face, and an elderly human couple who looked like they'd been waiting in that courtroom for days.

"Okay, that's it," I finally called. "I'm making for the fallback point. Retreat slowly once the rest of the people are through, or if you see anything nasty approaching."

The paladin nodded, so I turned and sprinted down the steps like an army of wights was chasing me. It wasn't hard to imagine, for some reason. Their inhuman cries had thickened, and if not for my armor it would have driven me to the ground in pain.

I wound down a flight of stairs, then another, and then a third. On the fourth revolution the stairwell was much longer, and descended into a far larger chamber. A tram tube stretched along the far side, and I could hear one rumbling closer.

Perhaps three dozen passengers paced on the landing platform, eager to reach safety, real or imagined.

A sleek white tram burst into view, each car shaped like part of a dragon so that it resembled one in flight as it prowled through the transparent tubes stretching off in a variety of directions, many deeper into the planet.

An unearthly glow came from inside the tram, and as it slid to a halt the would-be passengers suddenly decided they had elsewhere to be as they began sprinting in the opposite direction. Wights flowed through walls and windows and doors, all swarming toward the doomed passengers.

I looked away, and forced myself to scan the rest of the situation and find us a way out. There had to be something.

The Inuran soldiers had set up a defensive position in a gift shop with a single door and a single window. That made it a death trap in my book. Clearly they'd never played the tram level of Arena.

Beyond them I spotted a few equally doomed shops, but no better shelter than what they had. That didn't make it a good place to hole up. In fact, holing up would almost certainly get them killed.

I trotted over to the far side of the gift shop, and ignored the Inuran mages staring in my direction. Even the ones who hadn't removed their helmets were looking my way, instead of at the stairs where the army of wights would emerge. Not exactly the crack troops I'd fought on Jolene's cruiser.

"There!" I yelled, though I'm sure nobody else had any idea what I was talking out.

I'd spotted a maintenance hatch. Maintenance hatches ran parallel to trams, or at least they had on

Kemet. Almost no one ever went down there, which had made ours the perfect place for outcast kids to play without being harassed.

I turned back to the Inurans and adopted my most authoritative voice. "There's a maintenance hatch down there, and we need to keep moving. There will be almost no one in that tunnel, and right now being away from crowds is the smartest thing we can do."

An Inuran in a helmet shook her head, then rested the barrel of her spellcannon on her shoulder. "We're not abandoning a tactically fortified position. There are already salt lines down, and we have room for six more people. Everyone else...you're on your own."

Angry mutters grew in the surviving refugees, about twenty in total. I noticed that Aruni merely observed everything with a detached calm. He made no move to influence the situation either way, despite having enough authority to run things. He'd demonstrated that in the courtroom.

Only then did I realize I'd lost track of the minister. I scanned the crowd but there was no sign of her. Vee was tending to an older woman clutching her side, and didn't seem like she'd know where to find my missing charge.

I spun to rush back up the stairs, but Minister Ramachan was standing right behind me.

"You are a terrible bodyguard." The minister folded her arms. "You said we need to make for the tunnel, and you're talking sense. Get down there and scout the tunnel to make sure it's not infested. I'll wait here with Vee until your man Seket falls back. In the meantime I'll see if I can diffuse matters here."

I nodded, grateful for the sudden distraction. I hated making command decisions. Especially ones that endangered the lives of people I didn't even know, much less know their combat capabilities. A small part of me empathized with the minister. She'd shouldered this for billions, and now did so for a hundred thousand ragged souls.

I couldn't do it for twenty.

The armor hummed as I drifted into the air, then zipped toward the hatch I'd seen. None of the wights had made it to this side of the station, and none seemed to notice when I drew my pistol and void bolted the locking mechanism. There was no time for anything else, and I wasn't really worried about locking it behind us since most spirits can walk through walls.

Tension wrecked me as I slowly pried the door open and peered inside. I nearly lost my breakfast when a wan glow met me, but released a breath I hadn't realized I'd been holding when I saw it was soft magical lighting, and not the horrible spirit glow.

The tunnel was clear.

I turned back in time to see dozens of wights flowing down the stairs as Seket sprinted just ahead of them. There was no sign of his aura, and I doubt he'd cancelled it on his own.

Something stronger must be controlling those wights.

INTERLUDE II

Irala appeared on the *Word of Xal*'s bridge in an exhalation of air that popped both her ears. She should have been wearing her helmet.

The bridge stood empty, with the single spell matrix alone and unwatched. That would be one of many changes she'd have to implement, and soon. Security mattered. Not that the lack of it was his fault.

Jerek had surprised her in the most pleasant way that a son could.

He'd found his passion, as syrupy as that sounded. Her boy had settled into being a leader, though an inexperienced one to be sure. He understood magic, and how to surround himself with good people.

Once upon a time she and Dag had talked about how maybe he'd be the perfect mix of them both, and she proudly admitted he was. He would eclipse them both one day.

If she gave him enough time for that to happen.

"Guardian, get me an image of the *Inura's Grace* on

screen at full magnification." She began pacing as the screen flowed into the desired image.

A long sleek vessel like a carpenter's wedge glittered in the black, and even from this distance she could sense the wrongness. "Guardian, what can you tell me about that ship as it stands right now?"

"Congratulations on your promotion, Captain." Kemet appeared and his staff struck the ground once, and sent up a flurry of illusory sparks. "The vessel we are dealing with shouldn't be a warship. She might have been the *Inura's Grace* once, but no more. Inura designed her as a university where magitech could be experimented with, and ultimately mastered. This vessel glows with illegal necrotech. Someone has retrofitted her with a far more dangerous type of magic."

"What about the trade moon?" Irala tried, but her voice was a small, pitiful thing. "Did anyone survive on the surface? Is there a chance they're alive?"

"Officer Jerek lives." Kemet gave a broad grin, and delivered a pair of staff sparkles. "I will know the moment of his death. However, I can tell you little of his whereabouts."

If Jerek lived then perhaps Div did too. She stifled that hope. It could break her if she let it take root.

"Can we survive a similar blast to the one that hit the trade moon?" Irala began pacing once more, the instant she became aware she'd stopped.

"Unknown," Kemet admitted. The Guardian shook his scaly head. "Our limited defenses might block the primary beam, but the residual spirits would be loose on our ship."

Irala offered a reluctant nod. She stilled her pacing, and considered the problem. How did they survive? Firing first might be an option.

Then the answer presented itself. A cloud of dots on the holoscreen rose from the Inuran moon like flies from a corpse, startled into the air by the presence of a predator.

Most of the dots fled in the opposite direction, clearly making for deeper in the system where they could open a Fissure, or hide until the menace left. A good number stayed, however.

Tens of thousands of drones twisted into the air with one will like a mighty tendril extending from the moon. They flowed toward the necrotech ship, but the vessel answered before they could close.

Hundreds of menacing white fighters rose to oppose the drones, and the two fleets met midway between Great Ship and trade moon, littering the system with debris and explosions.

From the start the necrotech ships had the advantage. Each possessed pale wards that shunted away Inuran spells, while the Inuran drones lacked similar defenses. Irala knew it would only end one way, though the Inurans were certainly getting their spells in.

"It was a delaying tactic," she realized aloud when she saw the moon had begun to spin. A port on one side opened, and she realized it must be a cannon, easily a dozen kilometers across. "Guardian, monitor their attack. If they damage the necrotech ship, can we follow up with our own cannon?"

"Negative, Captain. We lack the magic for a fully

powered spell, and firing one would leave us defenseless in any case." Kemet's tail lashed behind him, as a cat's might. "We will be unable to resist if that vessel attacks us. It might be wise to flee."

Indecision paralyzed Irala as the trade moon fired its cannon. A spear of golden light, the heart of stars and gods both, slammed into a pale aura of wards that became visible when struck.

The wards crumbled, and the beam slammed into the side of the Great Ship, searing deep into the hull. Atmo, internals, and crew were flung into space, though the wound appeared superficial.

"Captain?" Kemet raised an eyebrow. "We're being hailed by the enemy vessel. It's identifying itself as the *Maker's Wrath*, and the captain gives her name as Necrotis."

"Accept the missive," Irala commanded in her most authoritative tone. She rose to her full height, which wasn't terribly impressive, but she drew upon the commanding air she'd perfected during her brief tenure as the headmistress of the academy.

A pale-faced beauty of Inuran lineage stared out at her, save that a simple ivory mask covered everything above the high cheekbones. Her garb was a simple black uniform, not unlike the blue ones they'd found aboard the *Word* in old officer's quarters. Long pale hair cascaded down her shoulders, delicate and fine in the way only an Inuran's could be.

"Ah, the mother." The woman inclined her head a fraction of a degree, regal and perfect in every way. "I see you've been given command. Tell me, mortal, do you wish to keep it? I could end your pathetic vessel right now."

"Whoever you are," Irala gave back firmly, "you certainly lack manners. If you have hostile intentions we will resist, and I think you'll find that we are stronger than you bargained for. Guardian, locate Headmistress Visala and teleport her to the bridge."

The air shimmered and warped before her, and a moment later a very irate old woman appeared, the woman whose job Irala had done when Visala had gone haring off for three years. They still had no idea why she'd left, or what the destination of her sabbatical had been.

Visala adjusted quickly, and sized up the situation before speaking, thankfully. She studied the holoscreen, and gave a start when she saw the woman standing there.

"Who are you, blasphemer?" Visala's eyes narrowed, and the ancient Wyrm's terrifying power coiled within her. "And why are you aboard my grandfather's vessel?"

"Oh, my word...is that little Visala?" The woman the Guardian had identified as Necrotis leaned toward the screen and delivered a cruel smile. "One of Inura's favored brats. A dreamer, just as he was. I still cannot believe you had the temerity to keep your own name. History might have forgotten you, but I have not. You can hide in plain sight no longer, coward."

Irala stifled the urge to ask how the headmistress knew this woman, but removed herself from their exchange, instead choosing to observe and learn what she could about both parties.

"I don't know who you are," Visala growled, "but

you've soiled my grandfather's legacy. We will not stand for it. You will find that this is very much a warship, and we are very much prepared for battle."

"Your threats are feeble," the woman thundered. "Witness the *Maker's Wrath* in all her glory, and then prepare yourselves. When the last Inuran breathes their final breath I will come for you."

Irala waved a hand and willed the connection to end. "Are you mad, Visala? We can't afford to antagonize them."

The screen shifted back to show the battle between the Great Ship and the trade moon. The sight of it left Irala bereft of all feeling. All hope.

The Inuran drones had all been destroyed, and the *Maker's Wrath* appeared untroubled by the minor damage from the trade moon's cannon.

6

As you've no doubt gathered I have played a lot of video games in my life. I mean, haven't you? Some of those games involved me sneaking or sniping, and I wasn't a bad shot...with a rifle and plenty of time to aim.

There was none of that, just a pistol and seconds to act.

A tide of undeath flowed down the stairwell after Seket, and in the middle of the pack towered possibly the most terrifying cyborg in the sector.

I'm not sure 'cyborg' was the right word. From the waist up it appeared to be a pale-skinned Inuran man, and when I say pale I mean pallor of death. From the waist down a harness with eight grisly legs clanked its way down the stairs. Each "foot" was a dragon's claw, and the joint connecting the legs to the body was some sort of femur.

The buzzing sharpened in my head, and my HUD updated to tag the cyborg with more data. Outlawed necrotech? That sounded bad.

Anyway, I was talking about video games, remember? Well, sniper I am not. I sighted down my pistol's short barrel, and poured a mixture of *fire* and *void* into the weapon. She hummed with pleasure as the spell discharged, and a moment later a ball of voidflame detonated in the first rank of spirits.

Two wights near the blast were destroyed, and some shrieked in anger, but the spell had little effect on the tide. Wights flowed around the blast and surged toward the gift shop.

Seket huddled protectively outside, with a cluster of civilians behind him. As impressive a figure he cut in that golden armor, I knew he didn't stand a chance.

"Vee, get your aura up. Lead the survivors to the access hatch," I roared, and sprinted to join Seket. "We're fighting a delaying action to the hatch. Hold the rear with Vee as long as you can. I'm going to get the minister down into the tunnel, and make sure they're not walking into an even worse situation."

"Captain," Seket snarled. He stabbed a gauntlet at the gift shop. "Those men and women cannot survive without our aid."

I risked a glance at the horde, who'd slowed outside Vee's aura, a handful of meters away. The necromancer merely waited, and watched as the golden aura shrank when Vee made for hatch, as I'd ordered. I followed her. "I'm sorry, Seket. We can't save them. Come on."

"You're sacrificing these people to buy time." Seket's voice had gone frigid. "Pawns in a game."

"No, they sacrificed themselves. We are not respon-

sible for them, and we can't protect everyone," I snapped
back as I hurried after Vee. Most of the civilians had
followed her, and I tried not to focus on the elderly
couple lurking behind the gift shop who'd refused to
budge. "We can't save anyone who won't come with us.
Staying here is death, and you know it as well as I do."

Seket's armored form hesitated...then he trotted after
me. The paladin said nothing, and I didn't force the issue.

Tense faces glanced over shoulders as we made for the
hatch, but while the tide of wights prowled at the edge of
Vee's protective aura, the necromancer lingered outside
the gift shop nearly fifty meters away. He was clearly
waiting for us to leave, so he could pick the soldiers off.

"Damn it." I hated morals almost as much as I hated
feelings. "Vee, stop when you reach the tunnel, and don't
go inside. We're sending the refugees in blind, so don't let
them go any further than your aura. Seket, you've got a
rifle in that pocket, right? Let's make a dead necromancer,
assuming that's what our buddy over there is."

"Yes, sir!" Seket's tone soared even as he snapped
open his void pocket and fished out a rifle that could have
come from an Inuran forge...millennia ago. The paladin
snapped the ancient weapon to his shoulder and had
already begun firing before I raised my own.

A spear of brilliant radiance streaked from the
paladin's rifle. The beam incinerated several wights in its
path before slamming into the true target. The necromancer watched calmly, but made no move to dodge.

The golden energy exploded brilliantly against a wall
of pale wards that became visible upon impact. At first

the necromancer's confidence seemed well placed. At first.

A rolling wall of nuclear flame washed through the sigils, and burned into the necromancer. He staggered backwards, and one of his legs sheered off in the blast. The others compensated though, and prevented him from falling as he skittered away.

The time it took to stabilize gave Seket an opening to line up a second shot, even as I was still taking aim. Another golden beam streaked out, and this one punched through the wards with little resistance, and cooked away everything above the grisly harness, what my suit had labeled necrotech.

"Are you serious?" I called as I shifted my aim and incinerated the closest wight with a void bolt. "All this drama about we need to run away and you just basically one-shot that guy?"

The paladin hadn't continued firing. He stood there frozen in his golden armor, his faceplate aimed at his rifle as if studying it. "I...Captain, my rifle is not capable of inflicting that level of destruction. There's no way I could have laid that menace low on my own. The Maker...aided me somehow."

Judge Aruni cleared his throat, and tapped a foot on the ground near the hatch. "Captain, it was my under-standing that we were evacuating. Do we really have time to debate the source of your companion's power? There are still thousands of wights."

I nodded wearily. Dozens of wights swirled angrily outside the salt lines the Inurans had erected. More swirled around Vee's shield, their wordless hatred terrifying in both purity and intensity.

"He's right. Seket, hold the rear. I'm heading down to step on any traps." I turned to the hatch and dove through.

Old me would have laboriously climbed down the ladder. New me jumped blindly, and used *void* magic to catch myself. Flying might be the most awesome part of magic—I won't lie.

My enhanced vision buzzed as I scanned the pregnant darkness. Eww, not a good analogy. The swelling darkness? The lurking darkness? Can darkness lurk? Turns out it can.

A thick pool of shadow rose up to block the musty corridor about ten meters ahead, and then the shadow pile grew malevolent green eyes. It wasn't a shadow at all. It was a Wyrm.

I noted an immediate and critical difference between Wyrms I'd encountered and this thing, though. "Uh, Vee? You're going want to get down here with that aura."

The Wyrm had jagged wounds down the side. Lethal wounds. The eyes weren't the only glow. Bits of spectral light leaked from the corpse's wounds.

My HUD flashed, and a tag appeared around the creature along with the same outlawed necrotech tag I'd seen before.

"What is that thing?" Vee landed below me in a crouch.

"My suit is calling it a soulshackled Wyrm. I'm going to keep it busy until Captain Inura can get here and one shot it."

A pleasant laugh bubbled out of Vee, and somehow made an insane situation a little more bearable.

Time slowed and the light flashed above us as Miri suddenly dropped down next to us, her armor aglow with gold and green sigils as she lithely drew her pistol. She even did the hair flip.

"You never paid me." She gave me a smile that said it wasn't credits she was interested in. Or maybe it was. I'm bad at that whole reading people thing. "In any case, if that dragon kills you, then I won't get a tip."

"Where did you go, Miri?" Vee interrupted suspiciously. "You disappeared in the courtroom, and I haven't seen you since."

"Ladies? Dragon?" I hissed. And waved the barrel of my pistol at the creature looming before us, though it hadn't attacked yet. "Can we compare notes after it's dead?"

"It's already dead," Vee pointed out helpfully. So helpfully.

"How long can you hold that aura?" I asked, changing the subject to something relevant to our immediate survival.

Behind us more and more people were filing down the ladder, and up above I could hear the whine of Seket's rifle-of-death. The minister began talking to the people in low tones, and guiding civilians as far from the looming battle as they could get. One less concern.

I didn't see Aruni, and hoped he was still up there with Seket. Maybe he was a mage. If not, hopefully he kept himself from getting underfoot. The very last thing we needed was to lose Seket, because the paladin had to go haring off after another civilian.

Heh, civilian. Like I was some badass merc.

"Light it up," I called once my aim had settled over the dragon.

It lurked well away from Vee's aura, maybe thirty meters off in the darkness.

"Yes," answered a cultured voice from the shadows, not far from the dragon. "Do go ahead and...light it up."

An intense spectral glow rose from the dragon, and from the necromancer next to him. The one Seket had incinerated could have been his twin, right down the eight scuttling legs with their disquieting bone and claws.

So we lit them up. Vee's bracelet came up, and Miri's pistol, and we emptied a fair number of spells into the dragon. Or tried to. A swirling wall of wards met our assault.

I blinked when I realized the necromancer had begun to hum. He sketched *spirit* and *water* sigils as he repaired the ward even as we struggled to take it down. His work eclipsed our damage. We couldn't get through.

"Are you quite finished?" The cheeky bastard called. "I can do this as long as you wish."

"I doubt that." I glanced through the hatch and smiled as Seket's armored form rolled through.

The paladin landed in a graceful crouch, then rose to his feet as he caught up on tactical.

"Can you wipe the smile off that guy's face, please?" I relaxed my grip on the pistol since the necromancer wasn't attacking.

"Oh, please," the necromancer called. "You think I

fear a spell from that puppy? Let him do his best, and then I'll give my little speech, and I'll let you get back to your day."

Seket roared as the rifle whined, and the same spear of light stabbed into the necromancer, in the same place. Layer after layer of wards were peeled away, but the necromancer's hands spun like a spider, and sigils swirled into place to repair the damage.

Seket fired again, and while he made it through a few more layers, they were repaired almost as quickly.

"Now then," the necromancer gloated. "I'll be on my way. I just wanted to leave you with this little fact. You already carry the seed of your own destruction with you. And I will enjoy watching it unfold."

Both dragon and necromancer faded into the darkness as they retreated up the tunnel just as suddenly as they'd appeared.

7

No one moved for long moments, and I suddenly realized they were waiting for me to say something. Even the minister was just standing in the corner with the shaken civilians, and Judge Aruni didn't seem in a hurry to take charge of anything but the corner he was standing in.

I did notice him eyeing me though. I glanced at my HUD, but the armor hadn't provided any additional tags beyond standard biometrics for an Inuran. Nothing about what kind of magic he might possess, if any. Either he was magically barren, or somehow he was hiding it. That didn't seem possible.

"Jerek?" Vee whispered over a private channel. "We need you."

She was right.

"Miri," I called loudly, through my suit's speakers. "You know this place better than the rest of us. We need to get to wherever your reactor is, and then find a lift to the surface. Or, if you know a better place where we can get to an uninhabited part of the surface we need you to take us there."

Miri tossed her hair over her shoulder like she'd been about to do it anyway, and held out a datapad to me. "I can do that, and I'll do it for free. But I do need to eat when this is all over. Would you mind taking care of the bill?"

"I thought your contract was with the minister?" I blinked at her. "You said she'd left you to wait for me."

"No, I said that she wanted you to follow her." Miri's smile softened the deception a hair, but only a hair. "I never said she'd hired me."

Vee raised her bracelet, and for a moment I feared she would cast a spell, but she settled for a harsh glare, then stalked up the tunnel, taking her aura with her.

"We're moving out, people!" I called, then turned to Seket. "Take up the rear. I'll walk with Vee and Miri on point."

"I'll get them moving." The paladin spun and approached the civilians, then thudded the butt of his rifle against the ground with a hollow boom. "On your feet, supplicants. Walk slowly ahead of me. Stay within ten meters at all times."

I considered asking the minister to pay Miri, but I hadn't even glanced at the bill she still held. Maybe I could afford it.

"Wait, all you get is sixty credits?" I blinked down at the price. I sketched in a 100% tip, and tapped accept. "You know what? Charge me for getting to the surface. How do you guys even make a living here? How many jobs do you have to do a day? I know people selling donuts who out-earn you."

I started into a fast walk, and Miri paced me as we moved to catch up with Vee, the refugees in tow. My suit insulated me from the smell, but I could see from the others' faces that we were passing through some rancid shit.

Dark stains covered the walls and floor, and stepping in puddles left your boots sticky for...well, mine were still sticky from the last puddle.

"Back there," Miri whispered as we walked. "Your artificer asked where I was. I've been shadowing you the whole time, and watching Aruni. When the Klaxon went off, just for an instant, his face...changed. He was someone else. Then he went back to being himself."

"I've noticed a few odd things as well," I whispered back as we fell into step with Vee. I raised my voice a bit for her. "We're talking about Aruni. My scans pick up nothing from him...no magic of any kind. He's ordinary in every way. Alarmingly so."

"I think you might be right. There are a lot of strange things going on, other than this moon being consumed by unclean spirits, like it deserves." Vee frowned at Aruni. She'd paused, which afforded the refugees time to catch up. Many were limping, though if any injuries were serious I was sure Vee would have tended to them. "The way Seket's blasts tore that necromancer apart? That raw power is beyond what his rifle should be capable of. It doesn't matter how strong the wielder is. The gun is limited by its own internals. It can only process so much magic. I can't explain what we witnessed, but I'm wondering if Aruni can."

"He can't be trusted," the minister whispered, close enough to my ear that I jumped. How had she approached so quietly. "Kill him, before he kills everyone."

"You want me to what?" A loud and poorly timed bang came from behind, and I spun to see an elderly man picking himself up from a collision with an overfull refuse canister. The minister helped him to his feet.

Wait, the minister was beside me, advising me to kill Aruni....

I spun, but the minister's double I'd just been speaking to had, predictably, vanished. I didn't know what it meant, and decided to keep the whisper to myself for the time being.

We continued slowly up the corridor, every step purchased with courage.

"So what do you guys think the necromancer meant? Why did he let us go?" Vee asked. Her aura still shone clear and strong, but I knew it couldn't last forever.

We'd need to get her a place to sleep before she could do it again, same with Seket.

"I think," I wondered aloud, "that he believes we'll tear ourselves apart trying to reach the surface. We carry the seeds of our own destruction." I left out that the seed might be a literal spirit. The timing of my nasty little figment couldn't be a coincidence.

Something was hunting us. But what did it mean? Was it a spirit? And, if so, why did it want me to kill

Aruni? Why not attack outright? I needed time, and Quantum, so I could research this thing.

"Jerek!" The minister's clear voice rang out. "Can we speak for a moment? Everyone? We need to decide where we are going to go, and what we are going to do."

I glanced down the access tunnel with my enhanced vision, but saw nothing dangerous. A glance in the opposite direction gave the same. We were as safe as we were likely to get for the moment.

I toggled the group-wide channel in my suit. "Set up a perimeter around the minister and her group. Let's get this sorted."

Vee nodded, but as she passed I noted a haunted expression. Something had spooked her badly, though I knew asking would be futile, even if we had the time to talk about it. What had she seen, or realized?

"We need to establish priorities," the minister's clear voice rang out. She seemed unsatisfied with her authority, and stepped atop a bench I wouldn't have used someone else's armor to sit in, much less mine. "Water and food will be critical. Shelter comes next. We cannot make it to the surface without resting, so our top priority should be capitalizing on any shelter we find."

I suppressed a twitch. The misuse of the word 'priority' triggers me. It's singular. You get *one*. By having three or more, as many people do, you have none. Which was more important? Food? Water? Shelter? Was intel a priority? I suffered in silence as the minister continued.

"I believe I saw a shopping assistant with Jerek." She scanned the crowd until she located Miri, and don't think I didn't notice that she didn't use my rank. Again. I might have passed the *Word* to my mother, but I still ran the *Remora*. "Ah, there you are. Can you—"

"I've already taken a job, I'm afraid." Miri duplicated her previous smile, a practiced tool in her arsenal. Also an effective one. "Captain Jerek has hired me to lead him to the surface, and I work for him."

"Ah. Are there any other, ah, personal assistants available?" The minister scanned the crowd, but no one stepped forward. Irritation marred her features. "All right then. Jerek, could you order your glom to locate a suitable place to acquire supplies, then a place to rest and tend to injuries?"

I didn't like the idea of taking orders from her, but everything she'd advised made great sense. Except for the insult to Miri. More and more I questioned Mom's taste.

"Miri, can you find us a place with a foundry that can replicate food and, ideally, salt?" That basically followed the minister's request, but made it clear the order was mine.

"Of course. There's a Supply Depot, one of our local chains, but it will charge us for everything we make. If we try to override the security...well, it's in a blue zone." She glanced at Judge Aruni. "You're rich, right? Do you have enough credits to purchase supplies for everyone?"

Again Aruni had been lurking in the rear of the crowd, as far from attention as he could get. Such a strange demeanor for a judge.

"We should murder them all," Aruni's cultured voice whispered into my ear, despite the clear impossibility since I was staring straight at the man. I glanced behind me, but there was no one there. No one visible.

I activated my sight, but no spirits were lurking. It might be possible they'd retreated into the spirit realm, but barring that I didn't see how I could have missed anything. Had that been Aruni using a spell? What possible motive could he have had? I turned back to hear his response to Miri's question.

"Yes, I am rich. I will pay for supplies. For everyone." Aruni folded his arms, and looked none too pleased by the prospect. "Get us to this facility and keep me alive, and everyone sleeps with a full belly, whatever medicine they might need, and appropriate gear to make it to the surface. We're all getting out of here. Together."

"Yeah that cinches it." Miri drew her pistol and aimed it at Aruni. "You aren't an Inuran judge. What are you? There's no way you'd help all these people without a deal in place first."

"I am an old man." Aruni shook his head, clearly disappointed as he strode to Miri until her spellpistol pressed up against his chest. "They'll ruin me for this, it's true. But I will get to do some good before my enemies exact the final price. It's time to come into the light, and to make some amends at the very end of my life. I am guilty of a great many crimes, but not whatever it is you think I've done."

Miri's aim faltered, and she abruptly holstered her pistol. "We don't age, so I'm not sure what you mean by the end of your life. All right. I'll accept you at your word, if my employer does."

"I do." I directed my attention to the minister. "Miri will take us to this Supply Depot. We'll move quickly, avoid combat, and rest when we get there. The longer we stand around here, the more likely something, or multiple somethings will find us. We need to keep moving."

Many of the refugees nodded at that, and irritation flitted across the minister's features. "Of course. Whatever you think is best in combat situations, Captain."

A victory, if a small one. I'd take it right then. Not all of us were going to make it to the provisioning station alive—of that I remained certain.

8

The trek to the Supply Depot was clad in grim silence and stoic resolve. We were hurting, but no one complained and no one slowed down. The horrors we'd glimpsed were tiny things besides the unknowns we conjured. Or that I conjured anyway.

That necromancer had spooked me badly, and the idea that some sort of spirit had grafted onto our group made things worse. Was it me or were people now eyeing their neighbors a bit more suspiciously? That had to be in my head.

Or was it? I badly needed sleep. Thinking had reached the blurry phase before monotone grunts, and my adrenaline was all used up.

"Contact!" Miri bellowed from about fifteen meters ahead. She dropped into a crouch behind a pillar. "I spotted three incoming."

My shoulders sagged wearily, and I longed to lay down. That seemed like a bad idea in a looming firefight.

"Seket, get the civilians to a safe distance." My pistol

slid into my hand and I trotted toward the pillar behind Miri's, about three meters away. "Vee, I need you up here."

Feet pounded on pavement, louder and louder until Vee slid into a crouch next to me. She hadn't put her helmet on yet, and her cheeks were flushed from the continuous exertion. Dark circles of exhaustion wreathed her eyes. "What did you need?"

"I'll go low and you go high. When the targets come around the corner, let Miri take her shot, then finish any wounded." I crept around the pillar and took aim with my nameless pistol. "You know what? Screw that. It's time for a name. Equalizer."

"Menacing," Vee said in a tone that promised it wasn't. "Get ready."

To my surprise the pistol gave an annoyed thrum in my hand. Guess she didn't like the name either.

I forced deep breaths as the targets came around the corner. I'm not sure what I expected. Wights. Zombies. Necromancers. That crazy dragon thing my suit had labeled soulshackled.

What I didn't expect was a trio of average commuter-mages in the tattered rags of what used to be business suits. All three frothed at the mouth, a sickly grey foam leaking out as hatred leaked from their eyes. Nothing human lurked there. Something alien, something that hated us all, stared back.

But they were alive. Their chests rose and fell like bellows as they charged toward us. There wasn't even a moment's hesitation. Their eyes landed on Miri, and they came for her.

We followed the plan.

Miri unloaded a pair of life bolts into the closest target, a middle-aged woman who'd kept her figure and her laugh lines. Each bolt caught a knee, and the suddenly legless woman toppled to the ground with an enraged cry.

Her companions leapt over her, and I timed my spell accordingly. "Old tricks are the best."

I launched a gravity bomb spell at the area where they would land, and as I'd hoped, both screaming commuters thrashed helplessly in their suddenly zero-g environment.

Vee sighted down her wrist, and delivered a pair of life bolts, one to the heart of each helpless target. They thrashed and wailed, then their bodies went limp.

Moments later a river of dark fog rolled out of both mouths, and coalesced into shadowy creatures that strongly resembled wights, but were shorter and more menacing.

Somewhere in the dim recesses of third year Arcana instructor Li's nasally voice reminded me that creatures not from our realm are vulnerable to their opposites, and to the other realms.

The opposite of *spirit* is *dream*. Did that mean I could use sleep spells to hurt undead? If so, why wasn't that, like, a thing that people knew and did?

Oh, crap...it *was* a thing that people knew and did. I just hadn't been one of the people.

The pistol hummed eagerly as I loosed a dream bolt at the first shade. The crackling pink beam slammed into the creature's midsection, and it gave the beginning of a shriek before the spell consumed it and left nothing but a few stray magical particles.

I adjusted the barrel a few millimeters to the right, and dropped the second shade with a similar bolt. Any celebration ended as I released my gravity spell and the pair of lifeless commuters tumbled to the wet pavement.

Miri ducked back into cover and cradled her pistol in both hands as she waited for the last target to advance. "You want to finish this, lurker girl?"

Vee's arm rose, her face locked in a mask of determination that made her impervious to the needling.

"No!" I raised a hand to lower her wrist. "We might be able to save them."

The last possessed commuter charged around Miri's pillar with both arms raised, fingers twisted into bloody claws that had already found at least one victim.

I snapped up my pistol and cast. The dream bolt caught the commuter in the side and the woman froze, then began twitching wildly. She collapsed and a low urgent moaning rose as the thrashing grew more intense.

Billowing vapor rose from the woman's mouth, and began forming another shade.

Vee's arm came back up, and the sigils on her bracelet flared. A beam of pure brilliance, the stuff of the universe itself, carried the shade back into the spirit realm where it belonged.

"Nice shot," I panted as I leaned back against the pillar.

Vee didn't answer, but instead rushed to the side of the downed commuter. She placed two fingers against the woman's neck, then looked up at me with a grin. "She's alive. Sleeping, from your spell."

"How about that," I murmured. "You can evict spirits with dream bolts."

"That's first year stuff," Miri pointed out as she approached. She rolled her shoulder, then knelt to pick up the unconscious woman.

"Yeah, even I know that," Vee pointed out. "The first documentary I watched on magic talks about realms and their opposites."

"I mean...you know what?" I holstered my pistol. "I'm just going to take point. Miri, see if you can find a civilian to carry that woman so you're free to relieve me. Vee, could you, ah, send me a link to that documentary when you have the chance? I might have blown off first year magical theory."

I started up the corridor and Vee fell in a pace behind me, her wrist ready to snap up if another spell were needed. She still hadn't put on her helmet, and I think I finally realized why. Mine dulled my senses. Sure, you had speakers, but you were divorced from the situation. You couldn't feel the air on your skin, and you only heard what the speakers did.

Anger marred Vee's features as she eyed me sidelong. "You had a chance to attend an academy, and you blew off your classes?"

"Yeah, basically," I admitted, and it hurt. "Briff and I really got into Arena. We were good, and we thought that maybe we'd even have a shot at going pro. I told myself that I already knew the magical basics, and for the most part I did. It's the gaps that might get me, or us, killed."

"That's why you hired me," Miri called from several meters back where she was passing her charge to a broad-shouldered Inuran woman who looked to play some sort of professional sport from her attire.

"How much further to the depot?" I called back as I paused next to the corner of a T intersection.

"A few hundred meters." Miri trotted up to join us, unwinded by carrying a human adult for a significant length of time. I'd have been panting, though proud that I could at least do it now. I noted she still had her spellpistol drawn. "Want me to resume point?"

"Do that. Vee and I will follow ten meters back." I leaned against the wall as Miri disappeared around the corner. She really enjoyed the respite, brief as it was.

"Do you really think Aruni will buy everyone water?" Vee whispered as she crouched next to me.

"They'll tear him apart if he doesn't." I rose reluctantly, and forced myself into motion around the corner. Vee followed, so I continued. "I think he'll deliver. I don't know what game he's playing, or why we can't piece together anything about his magic, but he does need us to get to the surface. If he betrays us I expect it will come when needs to make good on ruling in our favor against the Consortium. But if we're alive to be mad about it that's a win."

Vee nodded thoughtfully. "There's something about Aruni. He's hiding something, but I don't think he's malicious. There's something almost...familiar."

A shrill whistle echoed down the corridor, and I looked up to see Miri signaling us to approach. I did so, and summoned what alertness I could. Even with my vision it still wasn't easy. So. Tired.

I glanced around the wall where Miri crouched and blinked when I saw what had stopped her. A trio of steps ringed a raised building with nasty looking turrets dotting the roof. Those turrets were operating overtime, and with good cause.

Hundreds of wights surged toward the Supply Depot, right into the waiting embrace of those spellcannons, which lobbed explosion after explosion into their midst. Wight after wight died, and the cannons kept firing.

I rubbed my temples. "How do we get inside?"

"That's solvable," Miri offered, her attention on the building. "What I'm more worried about is in that window, there."

I followed where she pointed and spotted a pair of eyes staring back at me. I could see enough of the uniform to identify an Inuran security officer.

"Think they'll let us inside?" Vee asked, though hope had departed her voice.

"Nope." I drew my pistol. "But we're going to find a way in anyway."

9

I risked a quick look around the corner at the Supply Depot, then darted back into cover. This did not look good.

A quick survey of our resources dampened whatever withered remains of hope still lingered. Our mages were dry, and the people we protected were exhausted, hungry, and frightened.

"Seket," I whispered into the comm on a squad-wide channel. "How many spells do you have left?"

"Not many." He shifted in his armor, and his void pocket opened. The paladin dropped his rifle inside, and withdrew his blade. "I'm low enough that melee is probably the safest option. Besides, if we're rushing a door we want me in the van taking the brunt of it."

Seket snapped his wrist down for emphasis, and his blue-white spellshield flared to life.

Aruni surprised me by stepping forward and clapping Seket on the shoulder. "You are a credit to your god, young paladin. I am sure that wherever he is he must be proud of you."

In that brief instant something electric crackled between them. Something magical, but not a magic I recognized. It wasn't a spell in the traditional sense, but Aruni imbued Seket with...something.

None of my companions noticed, including the paladin, so that too was stowed for later. Another question Aruni owed an answer to. I turned to Vee. "How are you holding up?"

"I can fight." Despite her brave words and the set of that pretty jaw, I'm not sure I agreed with her assessment.

I studied the wights, who still piled into the line of fire as if gleefully seeking their own destruction. Each disappeared in a puff of dust, and the cannons simply kept firing. "Miri, the turrets must have rules on who they target. Will they shoot at us if we approach the depot?"

"It's possible." Miri's smile slipped for the first time. "If they've been set to free fire they'll attack everything. If not...then they are programmed to assault anything that's perceived as a threat. Carrying a weapon won't set them off. Having one drawn could. Firing one definitely will."

I glanced behind me at the minister and the other civilians. There was only one way to test this, and I knew it. We had to be certain before we risked everyone.

"I'll go. I can evac the quickest if it goes south." I steeled myself, then lunged around the corner and charged into a full sprint before anyone could protest.

No one did. Being leader sucked.

I poured on my meager burst of speed with my pistol in one hand. A half dozen wights broke off from the main tide and started in my direction. In response the closest spellcannon began its deep hum, and I winced as it discharged a spell that impacted behind me.

I glanced back and saw no more wights, though the rest of the pack had started in my direction. "Woo hoo! That's right. That's what you get!"

There was just enough time to turn, sprint a few meters, and start gloating that the spellcannon wouldn't shoot me when it hummed again...and shot me.

E tu, cannon? That's a quote from an ancient Terran emperor who got backstabbed by some guy named Brotus. They loved appending the word 'bro' to everything.

The humor stopped when a crackling ball of plasma caught me in the side and sent me careening into the corridor wall a good twenty meters from where I'd started.

A thick crack ran down my faceplate, and red flared in the torso and left arm on the paper doll. Worse, I'd dropped my pistol, which still lay where I'd been standing.

Did I mention the sea of wights screeching their way right over that location as they surged toward me? I closed my eyes and blinked to the steps outside the depot, but aimed the spell's destination at a spot that put me in the overlap of two turret firing lanes.

I appeared in a frosted heap on the steps, and took several heaving breaths as I adjusted to my new position. Panic rolled through me as I realized that my spellpistol, the pistol Vee had forged, no longer lay on the deck where I'd dropped it.

A dozen wights converged on my position and I forced myself to keep my eyes open, and to remain motionless as they approached. To my horror and delight both spellcannons on the roof above me opened up, and began torching the wights converging on my position.

Dozens of the things went down, until they were slowly forced back. I picked myself up, and as I did so gave a double take. My pistol was back in her holster. I hadn't told her to do that. Somehow she'd teleported back home, or walked over with feet I didn't see.

"I promise I'll give you a better name." I patted the weapon as I toggled on a squad-wide channel. "We're okay if we're armed, but not if we're openly carrying a weapon. Holster everything, and then approach me one at a time. I'll cover you from the steps where they turrets can't target me."

"Of course, Captain." Seket's sword went back in the void pocket, but he kept his shield out as he trotted toward my location. His journey did a lot less collateral damage to his armor.

Mine would heal, theoretically, though I wasn't certain how or even at what rate the armor healed. Back at the Academy they'd discussed magic items being life forms and healing just like us, but that was another area I didn't understand as well as I'd like.

Vee came next, though Miri began her approach a moment later and made sure to trot past Vee so she reached the other side first. Vee's eyes narrowed, but she refused to quicken her pace.

I heard a rattling behind me, and glanced back at the double doors, which were closed and barred. A narrow slit had opened across both, and four rifle barrels had emerged.

"Get down!" I roared, then dove for the wall out of their field of fire.

Seket bore the brunt of the assault, a mix of light bolts and explosive rounds. Each blow knocked him back a half step, and added another crack to his armor.

Then Vee was there. She stepped in front of the paladin and erected a swirling golden life ward, which intercepted the next volley.

Miri skidded into a slide that carried her to the doors directly underneath the doors. She grabbed a pair of barrels, and yanked them into the slots to disrupt their aim.

That gave me the perfect distraction, and I darted forward to ram the barrel of my pistol through the slot. I emptied a pair of high magnitude void balls at point blank range, and the screams inside stopped when the second one landed.

Seket charged the door, and lowered his shoulder at the last moment. Eldritch spellarmor met dirt cheap alloy with predictable results. Seket crashed through the doors in a shower of glass and metal...right into the sights of the waiting defenders.

Six soldiers opened up on the paladin, and his armor could only withstand so much. Twin roars of pain came from Seket as each of the final shots impacted, and he tumbled to the ground with the wreckage.

I had exactly one instant to figure out how to deal with all six guards. My gravity trick might get two. It might get four if I fired a pair of spells. But no matter how

I sliced it, two remaining guards would have me dead to rights.

Instead I cast darkness, a void power I hadn't yet found a use for. I'd never enjoyed being blind, and the fact that my opponent was also blind didn't help. In this instance, though, I still had my enhanced vision from the *Flame of Knowledge*. I could see through magical darkness. They couldn't.

Seemed fair to me.

I dropped to the ground as their next volley sailed harmlessly over me, then aimed carefully, walked my pistol down the line, and started kneecapping blind mages. Imagine my surprise when all six went down. It felt like cheating. Gotta be honest though. When I'm involved in something that can kill me I have no issue with cheating.

I climbed to my feet, and released the darkness as Miri joined me. "Can you cover them?"

She advanced with her spellpistol up. "They're covered. Tend to your paladin. Give that guy a raise."

I knelt next to Seket, and helped him get his helmet off. Sweat coated his hair into elegant coils framing a perfect face. "I'll survive, though my armor might not. Get the survivors inside."

I rose and turned back to the door. The civilians all waited in a cluster around the minister in the paladin-improved doorway. I waved her forward. "Go! Go! Get inside. We need to seal this place up."

That wasn't going to be easy now that Seket had introduced himself to the door.

Still, I focused on the positive. We were alive and had

made it to the depot. Now, if Aruni was as good as his word, we could get some food and some rest.

"That's why there were so many troops." Vee pointed at the far side of the room. A massive forge and foundry dominated one full wall. This place could print anything we could conceive of.

I was more interested in the couches against the wall.

10

I only really saw past the couches inside the Supply Depot once the battle had ended and the haze began to clear. Miri dutifully monitored our prisoners, though none made any attempt to stand or reach for a weapon.

Refugees threaded into the room in twos and threes, each darting a glance over their shoulder at the endless tide of wights feeding themselves to the turrets. If those turrets stopped working for any reason....

"Miri, how much do you know about the power source for the turrets?" I glanced through the shattered doorway as the last few stragglers made it inside.

"Not much." Miri addressed me without breaking eye contact with the prisoners. "They could stop at any time for all I know."

"That's unlikely." Vee's overpowering smugness was accompanied by an equally smug grin. "Guess the lurker girl will have to teach you some basic Inuran artificing. These turrets are in a blue zone. They're government property. Their runes will lead all the way back to the closest core. As long as that core is live...they'll keep firing."

"How do you know about blue zones?" I asked. When did she find the time?

"I read up on protocol for visiting merchants before we arrived," Vee explained in the kind of tone that made it clear I should have done the same. "Anyway, we're safe for now, unless something stronger comes. We have time to finish making supplies."

She nodded at the forge, which had been working overtime even in the few seconds we'd been inside the depot. Most of the initial requests were food, water, or both. Some were asking for weapons, and several people were carrying buckets of salt.

I didn't need to issue orders. People had already begun reinforcing the salt lines that had been damaged during the explosion, just in case a wight got past the turrets. We'd entered some sort of animal-brain survival mode where the tribe worked silently together for the good of everyone.

That gave me time to look around, and really see what this place was. Gambling machines lined the path to the credit console, where you could collect your wages for a nominal 23% fee.

I glanced at the running session total on the screen where Aruni stood. We'd already entered the thousands of credits, and I hadn't seen anything extravagant printed. I did some mental math. If Miri saved ten asses a day that was 600 credits, plus let's say 300 more in tips, because of that smile and also her ability to literally save one's ass.

So 900 credits a day. I glanced at the rations being printed, mostly soy products, though some people had used Aruni's generosity to forge real protein-based meat, or a birthday cake, in one case.

The birthday cake cost 120 credits. Soysteaks were 60. Those kind of rates kept these people broke and hungry, and siphoned up every spare credit they had into this depot. The genius and the cruelty were uniquely Inuran. Well, maybe not uniquely, but they'd certainly coined the current definition. I pitied Miri's situation, especially given how competent she'd proven.

"How do they get away with charging these prices?" I finally asked as I nodded at a wall full of illusory advertisements, most brightly colored, and at least half involving nudity, pasted right next to a 2 for 1 on ice cream.

"What do you mean?" Miri twitched a glance in my direction, but her aim never left her charges.

"On other sector stations they charge less than 20% of what you're paying here," I explained. "I fed myself on less than five credits a day back where I lived, and even living in nicer areas I wouldn't expect to pay more than 60 credits for a fancy dinner for two."

"It wasn't always this bad." Miri nodded at that, though she still eyed her charges. "I suppose it evolved over time. You've heard the ancient Terran analogy of the boiling child?"

"Excuse me?" I recoiled at that. "No, and I'm not sure I want to. That sounds barbaric. Who would do that? And why would someone repeat a metaphor about it?"

"Anyway." Miri bowled over my protests. "If you turn

up the heat quickly, then the child will climb out. If you sit in the water and they gradually raise the temperature, though, they'll stay in until they cook."

"No." I shook my head. "Just no. There's no way a kid would sit in a boiling pot. I'm sorry. Kids are way smarter than you give them credit for. The ancient Terrans wrote down some weird stuff, that's for depths damned sure."

"Well, flawed analogy or not, my point stands." She shot another brief glance my way, this one a tad annoyed. "They've slowly raised prices over my lifetime and there isn't much we can do about it. My parents say it was the same for them."

"You could get off this tomb," I offered. "If we make it to the *Remora* we'll get you off world, and if you can't find a place you're welcome to berth with us until you find something you like better. We aren't rich, but we eat well, and the pay is better than you get here. Plus we hit Catalysts."

"I don't think she should come," Vee protested. I thought she'd been using the forge, and turned toward her in mild surprise. Her eyes glowed with malevolent red flame, and a magical assault slammed into my mental defenses. The voice deepened and elongated into something sinister. "Kill her, Jer. Put your pistol to her temple and execute her. You'll never be with me otherwise. We don't need her, Jerek. Kill her. Be with me. Miri is in the way."

Rage rumbled out of the primitive parts of my mind, the demand that I take action now, no matter what that action might be. The rage had no source. I couldn't pin it to anything specific. Everything made me angry. Oh,

Maker, no...I'd become one of those frothing posters on
the Arena forums.

I wrenched my pistol from my holster and loosed a
dream bolt at malevolent Vee. The specter dissipated into
grey mist, and flowed away with a laugh.

My attention returned to the room around me, but no
one else seemed to have noticed phantom Vee. I activated
my vision, but no sign of the spirit remained. It must have
retreated to the spirit realm, or had some means of hiding
from my sight.

"Are you insane?" Aruni thundered behind me.

I turned to see him addressing Vee, who'd pried open
the console on the foundry, and was now preparing to
hack it.

"If you take those schematics," Aruni continued, "the
Consortium will never stop hunting you. Even after...
this...they will still send assassins. They do not allow
intellectual property to escape the depot."

"He's right," Miri confirmed. Her attention had
returned to the soldiers, who were making no move to
resist or escape. "Don't risk it, lurker girl. They'll come for
you hard if you give them reason."

"Oh, you'd love that, wouldn't you?" Vee rounded on
Miri, her face twisted into a snarl...of rage. Misplaced
rage? It didn't slow her down. "You prance in here in your
tight pants, with your...hair. It's unseemly. It's unfair. At
least I know how a magitech core works."

The taunt sounded ridiculous, but...it made me so
angry. Vee was angry at Miri. So we should kill Miri.
Everything else hurt to think about, but those thoughts
came easily.

A sudden roar from Seket interrupted the situation. One of the refugees had picked up a guard's spellrifle, and delivered a life bolt to the paladin's back at close range. The drifter assailant screamed incoherently. "Dagoztookallzabeer, man!"

"You know what we need?" I called loudly enough to overpower the various conversations. "Sleep."

I calmly drew my pistol again and tagged the drifter with a dream bolt. Then I walked my pistol through the room, shooting anyone I thought might be a threat. I mean, they were angry too right? I couldn't take chances. It had nothing to do with me enjoying them slumping to the ground, prey before the superior hunter.

Wait, what? What had that thing done to me?

"Oh, well." I kept emptying dream bolts into my companions until something hit me from behind and everything went dark.

INTERLUDE III

Briff already hated being in charge of the *Remora*. Acting captain felt like a sham, because he'd never commanded anyone to do anything. He just happened to be the most least qualified person, so Jerek had left him in control. If Dag had still been around, Jerek would have made him do it.

Briff missed Dag. The old man had been a real bastard to Jerek sometimes, but he'd also done his best to help keep Jerek alive and make sure that Jerek had the skills to do it himself.

"Hey, Scaly," Rava called playfully. "You want to play a few matches since we can't get any sleep?"

Briff considered that. He liked gaming, and it might keep them awake, but it would also distract them. His tail drooped, and he shook his head. "We'd better stay alert in case we get attacked. I want Kurz to be fresh in case we need him."

"You don't need me fresh?" She raised an eyebrow that reminded him of Dag. "I'm your best merc."

That caught him off guard. He valued Rava. A lot. He didn't want her thinking he thought Kurz was better or anything.

"That's not it." He moved to stand by the holoscreen, which showed the starport where they'd landed. No ships had come or gone for hours now, and the ghostly glow had faded. "I need you ready to pilot. If we have to take off, you're our best chance. If you can't do it I can ask Kurz, but...."

"I'll do it," she confirmed. "But it won't come to that. If we get attacked we'll use the ship's spellcannon to drive them off. This thing is a fortress, and the hull is a magical alloy. Spirits can't get inside. Or at least...I don't think they can."

Briff's wings drooped. That wasn't reassuring. What would Jerek do? He'd make everyone feel like it was okay, and that he had a plan. He'd tell them what the goal was, and then he'd tell them a next step.

What was the goal? What was the next step?

Briff wanted to pick up Jerek. He needed to hold the landing zone until Jerek got here. No, that wasn't right. He needed to keep the ship safe, and be ready to respond to Jerek when the captain finally checked in. This might not be the LZ.

He forced his wings erect and proud, and tried to look a proper dragon. "We'll try to hold the LZ, but if we can't we need you ready to fly. At the first sign of enemy engagement I'd like you get in the matrix and pilot the ship."

Rava shifted uncomfortably, the leather of her jacket

creaking loudly. "I'll do what I can, but if we have to lift off I'm not responsible for what happens."

"I know. I am taking responsibility." Briff's tail swished powerfully behind him. "We'll let Kurz sleep until we need him, but I don't want to rely on the point defense cannons to defend us. We need you on that spellcannon in case something nasty shows up."

"You're right." Rava rose from the couch with a stretch and a yawn. "I'll get my comm unit and go hang in the matrix just in case. You wanna join me on the bridge?"

"Yeah." Briff took the lead and walked down the single corridor running the length of the ship until it reached the spacious bridge. He offered a toothy smile when Rava ducked into the matrix. "I really like the new ship better than the first version. This holoscreen is awesome, and so are the point defense cannons. We didn't have anything like this on the derpy version with the regular drive."

Rava laughed at that. "You've got a great sense of humor."

Briff turned back to the holoscreen, and peered out at the spaceport where they'd docked. They were reasonably safe in that they were at the end of the concourse, one of the last ships docked. The tide of spirits that had slammed into the planet hadn't yet found this area, and he hoped they never would.

Something clattered behind them, and Briff spun to see Kurz stumbling onto the bridge, his hair askew from sleep. "They're coming. Thousands of them. I can feel their approach. Closer every moment. The pain. The rage...it's incalculable."

"Um, do you think we should flee?" Briff's tail came around instinctively and he clutched it in both hands.

Kurz adopted a thoughtful expression. Or at least Briff thought it was thoughtful. He had trouble reading human faces, which was difficult when everyone you hung out with was human.

"If we do we'll have to find some other place to pick up the captain." Kurz scrubbed fingers through his auburn beard. Briff rather liked the color of his mane, though it looked better on Vee. "What do you want to do?"

That was the real question. What did he want to do? If he stayed they were a fallback for the captain. That was good. But if they got overrun that didn't matter. He turned to Rava.

"Can you pilot the ship?" Briff asked it plainly, though he hated that kind of confrontational question. "I mean really fly it. If you can, then we can lift off safely, and then wait for Jerek to contact us. We'll just go wherever he's holed up."

A low screeching rose in the distance, and a spectral glow crept onto the holoscreen as the horde clawed their way closer.

"I'm a fast learner." Rava rose to her feet. "I guess I tap the *fire* sigil on all three rings since I have *fire*." She did that, her fingers flying over the rings with all her usual grace. "Whoah...this is weird. I can feel the ship. Feel the drive."

The ship rumbled as the spelldrive roared to life, louder than when Jerek flew it with *void*, or Seket with *life. Fire* wasn't as good, but it still worked in a pinch, especially in an atmosphere.

"I really wish I'd been with you guys when you got *fire* magic." Briff's tail drooped. "I feel like all dragons should be able to breathe fire."

The *Remora* lurched as it ripped free of the station, the docking clamp still attached.

"Oops." Rava winced in the spell matrix. "In my defense no one mentioned I had to unhook anything first."

An irate and half-asleep soulcatcher stumbled into the doorway.

"You are not filling me with confidence," Kurz snapped. His hands trembled, and the room around him thickened with the acrid stench of human fear. Briff hated it.

"Kurz, please return to your quarters and try to get some rest." Briff rose to his full height, his go-to move when trying to appear intimidating. "Rava will get us where we need to go, but if we have to save the captain we'll need you fresh and ready to fight. Please."

"My sister's out there." The words had the sound of an apology. "I'll get some rest. Good luck, Rava."

Kurz headed back up the corridor toward the crew quarters, and Briff focused his attention on Rava. He shared Kurz's fear, but one of the things he'd noticed about Jerek is that he never showed a lack of faith in his crew. Jerek always made you feel like you could get it done, and he'd be right there helping you. He'd always been that way.

Briff wouldn't let him down.

"You've got this, Rava." Briff walked over and sat down next to her matrix. "By the time you pick up Jerek I bet you'll be a better pilot than he is. He'll be so pissed."

"Yeah!" Rava gave him a roguish grin. "I'm going to see if I can work out some of these systems. I'll keep us hovering. I can do that for a loooonnng time. We should be safe, but maybe keep an eye on the holoscreen? If something flying or with a ranged attack wanders up let me know and I'll get us out of there."

Briff's tail swished back and forth behind him. They could do this. They'd be here when Jerek called, and they'd do some epic combat drop to pick him up.

Somehow this was all going to work out.

He glanced up at the top edge of the viewscreen, and noted the Great Ship still hovering there, fresh from its victory over the Inuran fleet, paltry as it was.

That wasn't his problem. Jerek would handle it. All Briff had to do was get Jerek.

11

I came to with a gasp, and instinctively rolled. It saved my life as someone planted a spellaxe in the area I'd just occupied. The weapon crackled with air magic, and I scrambled backwards as I attempted to understand where I was and what was happening.

A life bolt took my assailant, one of the Inuran soldiers, in the side of the head, and I turned to see Miri give me a nod. That jogged a few things loose.

I'd been in the Supply Depot. Some asshole had clubbed me on the back of the head hard enough to knock me unconscious even though I'd been wearing my helmet.

The paper doll confirmed that, and I noted several red spots now. My armor was in rough shape, and I needed to avoid any direct engagements for another day or three. I wish.

Pandemonium had overtaken the place. Refugee fought refugee, and the Inuran soldiers had joined the fray as well. Miri's rifle whined several more times in rapid succession as she dropped the other soldiers who'd risen, one after another.

I activated my vision, and scanned for the spirit I now knew had caused this. There! A hazy grey blob with toxic green eyes stood next to the minister, whispering to her. As it did so, tendrils of milky-grey sigils swam into her ear and disappeared from sight.

The tendrils were everywhere, swirling in little clouds around everyone, myself included. I could see the ritual enchantment now, painstakingly woven by whatever this spirit was. We were witnessing the culmination of many hours of spellcasting, and something told me that if I couldn't end this creature and do it now all of us would be dead in a few more minutes.

Rage boiled in me. Rage at the spirit. Rage at my friends. Rage at the fact that numbers existed. Rage that my breath stank of stim drinks, and I had no access to a toothbrush.

Someone needed to pay.

I whipped my pistol up quickdraw style, exactly as my father had drilled into me. In a life and death situation speed matters, and if you couldn't do it fast enough, then you died.

My pistol came up and the weapon's magic stirred, steadying my aim. I poured the last of my *dream* into the weapon, and it discharged a high magnitude bolt of purple-pink magic.

The spell slammed into the spirit, which shrieked in agony, then wormed its way into the deck. It wasn't metal it tunneled through, but rather the veil between our realm and the spirit realm. As it slipped away I realized it had a way to come and go freely from the spirit world, but I could see the holes. I could be ready when it came through.

Except that I didn't have any more *dream* magic. I'd been running on fumes for a while, and my dream bolt marathon had taxed the last of it. If that thing came back I wasn't ready to fight it.

Worse, the pandemonium continued unabated. People still fought, though a few had shrugged off the effects. Vee among them. That boded well for our side.

"Vee!" I whispered into the comm on a private channel. "We can't stop the spell directly. I've hurt the spirit and it fled into the spirit realm. I'll keep an eye on it, but I'm low on magic. Can you be ready to life bolt this thing when it comes out? You're a better shot than I am."

"Not by much," she countered. "How am I supposed to see the spirit?"

"Good point." I still had a decent amount of *void* and some *fire*. I used *void* to blink over to her location on the far side of the room, a sheen of frost briefly coating my armor as I exited the heat-starved Umbral Depths. "I'm right behind you. If I spot the spirit I'll call out the location, and I'll tag it. Do your best to hit the same spot, and hopefully we can finish this thing."

I leaned against the wall with my pistol raised. I couldn't ignore the tremble in my hands, and knew it would effect my aim. Exhaustion could only be combated for so long, and my body was well past its limits.

The chaos around us lessened as fights were decided, or as the final survivors threw off the effects of the spell.

I took a moment to study that and realized many of

the clouds of sigils had begun to unravel. The spell likely required close supervision, and it appeared that if not tended to it would dissipate rapidly.

The spirit had to know that, which meant....

A hole opened directly between my feet, and I tumbled forward out of the way. By the time I came around, the spirit had emerged, and I tagged it with a void bolt. It screeched as spectral motes were ripped from its form, but kept coming.

Vee's bracelet came up, and the sigils flared as she released a life bolt. It grazed the spirit's shoulder, but did no real damage.

"A little to the right!" I yelled as I scrambled backwards on all fours, wishing I had time to regain my feet before that thing got ahold of me. Possession was the very last thing an exhausted mage wanted to wrestle. If that thing overcame me...well it would be ugly for my friends.

Vee's bracelet shone again, and a bolt streaked into the spirit. It howled in agony, and turned to face Vee.

I shot it in the side with a void bolt, then another.

Vee fired two more life bolts, then Seket was there with his spellrifle, adding more magical destruction to our volley.

The creature gave a final agonized shriek, then dissipated into a cloud of spectral motes as its form was drawn into the spirit realm.

"Will it be back?" Vee asked. "I don't know much about the ways of spirits."

"No," I promised as I holstered my pistol. "We bled away its power. There is a tug in the spirit realm, drawing everything there towards oblivion, as I understand it. If you beat a spirit they don't have the power to return here, unless someone summons them, or they find a hole in the veil."

That had about exhausted my knowledge of spirits, courtesy of a semester spent trying to impress a crush who'd loved the lore around spirits. She found it romantic and tragic, and I totally dodged a spell there, trust me.

"Well done, Captain." Aruni nodded at me from the corner where he'd weathered the chaos. He'd suffered no damage. Not even a torn garment. He still appeared as fresh as we'd seen him back in that courtroom. "The creature you killed was called a spite. They are drawn to *spirit* Catalysts, and are a favorite tool of necromancers."

"You know what? That would have been really good to know about three hours ago." I stifled the rage, which was easier now that it wasn't magically reinforced. "Why do I get the feeling you know a lot more about this situation than you've been willing to share?"

"Because you are perceptive." Aruni folded his arms, and regained some of the authority he'd cast aside. "I need you to get me to the *Remora*. If you can get me to safety, then I promise to not only make good on my agreement with your minister...who is unconscious, by the way. In any case I will also give you what you crave, Jerek. I will give you answers."

You can guess how I reacted to that.

12

Once I'd agreed to get Aruni to the surface I decided to take the man up on his generous offer.

The forge still worked, and Aruni still had his access code. I hadn't had my turn to look through the digital catalogue, and now I could thumb through almost every conceivable product line. It was like having the everything store right next to you.

And the prices reflected that.

Each time I added something to the cart I winced. I mean how could I not when I'd just spent 1,200 credits for a week's worth of "premium rations," whatever that meant. It helped that they weren't my credits. Aruni certainly didn't seem to care, as he stared through the missing door out into the street.

What else did I need or want though?

"You know there's a line behind you, right?" Vee rested a hand on my shoulder. "I need to get some grenades, and a change of clothes. I'm going to take one of the suits of spellarmor from the dead Inurans. It beats this environmental suit."

I nodded at that, again shocked by how callously her culture treated things like death. Sometimes I envied their pragmatic approach, but right now it just horrified me. We'd killed guards who were simply trying to keep what they had, and saw us as looters. The fact that we'd been attacked first gave us the high ground, but it didn't mean these people weren't just caught in a bad place at the wrong time.

"I'll let you know when I'm done. I approve of grenades." Which of course made me thumb to that part of the catalogue. I leafed through until I found what I was after. "There we go. I'm getting some pulse grenades."

"Spirits aren't affected by concussive blasts," Vee pointed out. I rather liked having her that close, and enjoyed her arm draped over my shoulder.

Miri might have been more classically attractive, but there was just something about Vee...the way we settled into a conversation.

"Necromancers are just as vulnerable as we are," I fired back. "We already have lots of ways to deal with spirits, even with our limited resources. We need more ways to disable spellcasters from range, and I can teleport these babies wherever I need them with perfect accuracy."

Eight small grey spheres appeared on the forge's tray, and I scooped them into my pack.

"Anything else or can I take a turn?"

I considered that. I wasn't going to be pressured out of making cool stuff. Not even by Vee.

"Yeah." I gave a grin and thumbed to conventional rounds. "I just remembered something I saw in an old holo I used to watch."

I'll admit I was mildly surprised when the catalogue had exactly what I was looking for. I ordered eight magazines of salt rounds, inventive rounds designed to take down spirits.

"What are those?" Vee nodded at the ammo as I scooped six magazines into my pack and pocketed the other two.

"Salt rounds have a sensor that can detect spirits," I explained as I withdrew the explosive rounds and replaced them with salt. "The sensor detonates the charge in the round, which creates a cloud of salt that disperses spirits. If you hit one they take damage, and can't reform for some time. From what I gather it only works on weak stuff, but hey...better than what I had."

"Smart." Vee sounded genuinely impressed, and squeezed the armor before she let me go. She dropped her voice a bit. "Hey, I wanted to say I agree with asking Miri to join the crew. I mean, not that you asked my opinion. She's a terrible person with the morals of a starved drake, and we will *never* be friends, but she's a great fit and has skills we need. I bet she'll get along with your sister."

The sudden acceptance took me aback.

"She's been more than a little terrible to you." I holstered my pistol. We had a ways to walk, and I could draw quickly enough if I needed to. "I'll talk to her about that. If she's going to come with us."

"Then what?" Miri asked as she strode up to the forge.

"Oh, we're doing this I guess. Okay." Lack of sleep made words difficult, but I took the time I needed to assemble them into the proper order. "You need to be nicer to Vee. She's an important part of our crew, and she's probably the smartest person I've ever met."

Vee gave a quiet squawk of indignation as if I'd accused her of something. I did not understand her as well as I thought I did.

"Okay, lurker girl." Miri nodded, then extended a hand to Vee. "We're on the same team, and I'll treat you like a teammate. You stab me in the back, and I will tattle. Promptly. But that will be the end of it. I don't want trouble, and I'm sorry if I hurt your little feelings."

Vee stiffened at that, and violence filled the air between them, making things electric.

"You're a mannerless trollop, but at least you make me feel like the cultured one. Apology accepted." Vee nudged me hard with her shoulder. "Now get out of the way so I can make stuff."

"Okay, okay." I stepped aside, and let Vee take my place as I headed to a quiet table. The entire depot was quiet now that most of the occupants were dead. That gave me time to do something I'd been meaning to since we started running. I keyed a missive through the spellarmor, and waited impatiently for it to connect.

"Jer!" Briff's scaly smile filled my HUD. "You're alive. I knew you'd make it. Where are you? We can come pick you up."

"We're beneath the surface. Are you still near the LZ?" Relief swept through me as I realized they were okay.

"I'm flying the ship," Rava yelled from off screen. "Better than you, little brother."

"Oh, Maker, help us," Seket whispered under his breath.

"We're right over the LZ," Briff said, still smiling. "If you can reach the surface and send us coordinates we'll come pick you up. How else can we help?"

"That will do it, really. We're going to make a run for the surface. Have you talked to my mom?"

"No, but I saw her shuttle reach the *Word of Xal*. I think she's okay, as long as that necroship thing doesn't fire on her."

"If she contacts you tell her that the minister was knocked unconscious, but that she's alive and well."

I didn't mention that when I said unconscious I meant I'd dream bolted her in a furious rage. I really didn't need the lecture that kind of incident would generate. I could hear it in my head now. *Now, Jerbear, I know that you don't like that mommy's dating someone new, but you have to put aside this anger.*

I slung the minister's unconscious body, which had been politely deposited in a comfortable chair I might add, over my shoulder. Gently. She didn't stir and I saw no reason to wake her. If I could keep her asleep until we reached the ship that wouldn't be the end of the world.

I didn't like having my hands occupied though.

Yet I had to admit that I'd be the best choice to carry her. Vee was a better shot than I was, and Seket a better overall fighter. I scanned the room, and steeled myself against the carnage.

Almost no one else had survived. Even Sarkor had

been cut down in the crossfire, the smug Inuran's face made handsome in death.

But of course Aruni had escaped without a scratch. Or a sweat stain.

"You have some explaining to do." I knew my tone was accusatory. "And I'll accept that you won't do it until we get to the *Remora*. But if you have anything, any scrap of knowledge, that can help us get there...please tell me now."

Aruni shook his head. "I don't have any specific information that will help us, but if I think of anything I will let you know."

His tone seemed genuine, and I was too exhausted to question it. If only there were a back room with a cot where we could nap for eight hours. Of course, laying down anywhere meant never getting up again.

We had to get off this moon, and if we didn't do it soon the lot of us would become a permanent fixture.

I hefted the minister over my shoulder, and tried to ignore the chattering of the spellcannons as they laid into the endless wights. Now or never. I walked out of the shop and into the street leading back to the lift, our destination.

Two necromancers with the same skittering legs patrolled the street in the distance behind the wights, but didn't seem aware of us. I waved at everyone to follow, and we crept around a neighboring building.

If we could make it to the lift, maybe we could reach the surface. "Miri, can you get us there quietly?"

She nodded wordlessly, and took point. Vee fell in behind her, then Aruni, then me, and of course Seket in the rear. His armor whirred and clanked, and every step sent echoing cracks down the pavement.

I summoned a bit of *void*, and levitated him into the air, then maneuvered myself behind him to grab his arm with my free hand, the minister still slumped over my other arm. "I can make this faster and quieter."

We hummed along more quickly, and Miri guided us down a series of alleys and access tunnels that skirted the main areas on this level of the moon.

My spirits even began to lift, but the moment they did I knew something terrible was about to happen.

We came around another corner, and saw the stuff of nightmares. Two dozen corpses littered the concourse leading to the lift, and every last scrap of their flesh had been eaten away.

An awful clanking came from out of sight, and we froze until the creature emerged into view. A quartet of skulls stared in our direction, each backed with the same spectral green glow and attached to a similar long prehensile neck.

As I watched, the creature knelt over one of the skeletons, and black tendrils extended from its body and picked the bones up, then grafted them into the body, increasing its size.

A terrible inhuman wail burst from every mouth, and the creature started toward us in a lumbering run.

13

My pistol came up and I loosed a fire bolt, since I was running low on *void*. The flame liquified the front foreleg, and the creature tottered right into Miri's life bolt.

Seket charged forward, then dropped low and sheered off the other foreleg, while Vee circled wide and peppered the creature with life bolts of her own.

That seemed to piss it off. All four skulls faced different targets, and I happened be one of the lucky chosen. I'd dropped the minister behind me, but not far enough away to avoid whatever this thing was doing.

There simply wasn't time to react. A spectral glow built in all four throats, and a ghostly bolt erupted from each. Mine sailed into my chest, and if my armor offered any protection I couldn't tell.

My very soul eroded as the *spirit* crackled through my body. Smoke rose from my nostrils and the corners of my eyes...yeah, that wasn't alarming. I shook my head and raised my pistol for another shot, again aiming for a leg.

The pistol added its own magic, and the enhanced *fire* built into a towering inferno that roasted the final leg to ash and spilled the creature to the ground.

In that terrible instant I realized it wasn't a creature. It was creatures. A sea of tiny black insect corpses scuttled away from the bones, abandoned as they swarmed toward me and my friends.

"I get the feeling we know what happened to the flesh on those bones," I muttered into the comm. "Fry these things. Do not let them reach us."

I unleashed a cone of flame from my pistol, which cooked the insects carpeting the ground before me. More swarmed forward, and I fired again. As I did so I noticed that some of the insects hit by the first spell were clambering to their feet. Damned these things were tough.

Miri and Vee were peppering the creatures with life bolts, but we simply couldn't inflict enough damage to stop them all.

I used the last of my *void* magic, and levitated all of us into the air. If I was wrong, we were in terrible danger, but if I was right, then the insects couldn't reach us.

A tendril rose from the floor, but fell short of reaching my foot.

"How did you know?" Vee asked. "And what if they figure out a way around it?"

"The bones," I explained as I drifted over and pushed Vee into Seket, then into the minister until we were one awkwardly flying ball. Miri managed to kick off a wall, and floated in our direction. "I think they eat the flesh to survive, and take the bones to give them structures to work with. Whatever they are, there's *spirit* magic in them. I can see it."

Another writhing tendril lashed up at us, but gave up and sank back into the mass when it too failed to reach us. The bugs swarmed toward the abandoned bones, and erected them into a creature once more.

I dropped the levitate. "Run for the lift!"

We sprinted before the bugs, and covered the thirty meters to the lift before they'd finished the hellish transformation back into an undead creature, this time with only one skull.

The thing lumbered in our direction, and I stabbed the button on the lift. "Come on, come on."

It picked up speed as the doors began to open, and I used my last *void* spell to launch a gravity bomb in its path. The creature's body flowed around the affected area, which took time.

Yes, I know I already said I'd used the last of it. I'm dramatic. Sue me.

We piled into the car, and Vee stabbed the button labeled surface. Panic rolled off us in waves, all save Aruni who moved to the lift's rear corner and waited passively with his hands clasped together.

The doors closed, and I finally exhaled when we whirred into the air.

"That was too close," I panted, and willed my helmet to slither off. It was the first time I'd tasted station atmo since I'd arrived.

"It isn't over," Aruni muttered in his corner. "The bone thief still pursues us."

"You mean it's climbing up the shaft?" Miri asked. She'd holstered her pistol, but drew it again.

"Precisely." Aruni hadn't budged a millimeter, and made no move to prepare a defense.

"I hate this moon so much." I dropped to my knees, then whispered a weaken miracle. A small section of the lift floor flaked and crumbled away, allowing a whooshing wind into the car. I peered through and paled at what I saw. "It's climbing the cables. We need a steady shot on this, and I'm all but out of magic. Who wants it?"

"I'll take it." Vee moved into position over the hole, the wind kicking up strands that had escaped from her auburn ponytail. She set her stance and aimed her bracelet through the hole. "I see it. I'm going to let it get closer before I take the shot. I don't have much juice left either."

We waited tensely, and about fifteen seconds later her bracelet flared and a beam of pure golden brilliance streaked through the hole I'd made. A frustrated cry came from below.

Vee fired another spell, and I noted the sheen of sweat along her brow. No scream accompanied this spell, but Vee still aimed, so she hadn't killed it.

"Out of the way, lurker girl." Miri nudged Vee aside, though gently at least. "I've still got a few spells. I can take this."

Vee's face became an emotionless mask, and she stepped aside.

Miri dropped to one knee and sighted down her pistol. "You really messed that thing up. It's slithering up the cables now, and the bones are gone. I can shave some of them off, but what we really need—"

"Is fire." I knelt next to her. "I can deal with them, but not until they're almost close enough to get in. And to be honest I don't know what my spell will do to the cable. If I make it low magnitude it won't kill the bugs."

"It will still knock them off," Vee pointed out. She knelt next to the minister. "I'm going to wake her, just in case we need to climb out the top or something."

I tuned her out, and focused on the shot. My cone extended about fifteen meters, and the bugs were maybe twenty-five meters away. I nearly loosed the spell when the first bugs made it in range, but forced myself to wait until all of them were within range.

"Maker please bless this shot." I squeezed the trigger, and gasped when a river of blue flame came from my weapon.

The fire flowed as if alive, and twisted around the cables to destroy the bugs, but not to harm the thick rubber that would send us tumbling to our deaths.

"How?" I held up my pistol and eyed her suspiciously. "Was that you?"

There were no words, but I could sense an empathic response. She seemed as surprised as I was.

"That was incredible." Miri delivered one of those smiles, but this one seemed tailored just for me. "I've never seen that kind of spell mastery."

I holstered my pistol and stared Aruni directly in the eye. "Neither have I."

Aruni offered an innocent shrug that seemed anything but. He was saved from further explanation as the lift rolled to a stop. Aruni withdrew a slender helmet from within his jacket and affixed it over his head where it connected with a slender suit of spellarmor I hadn't even realized he'd been wearing

My hand hovered over the button to open the doors, but I glanced around first to make sure everyone had their helmets on. The concourses on the surface might still have atmo, but we couldn't count on that.

The minister's eyes fluttered open a moment later. She'd missed the entire ride up.

"What happened?" The minister sat up and probed a knot in her forehead with a finger.

"Here, put this on." Vee handed the minister her helmet, and the woman's training took over.

The minister quickly sealed it over her head, then rose to her feet, all business now.

"We'll explain later. We've got immediate problems." I indicated the concourse outside the lift.

Hundreds of spectral faces were turning in our direction.

14

I slipped into Arena mode as the doors opened, and directed the squad like we were moving onto an unfamiliar level. Somehow that divorced me from the situation, and let me focus on what we needed to do. "Seket, you're on point. Vee, Miri, take up covered positions flanking him. Minister, put yourself up against the lift's wall, and don't come out until the shooting stops."

My people moved with a purpose, and it made me inordinately proud to see how well they performed. Seket swept outward with his shield held high and blade at the ready. Wights and walking corpses called shamblers began making for him. You've seen shamblers in every horror movie. They shuffle and try to bite you, and also they're dead, so don't let them.

Dozens of the things shuffled toward Seket, who'd knelt and begun pouring salt from a vial into a ring around him. It wouldn't stop the shamblers, but it would prevent the wights from touching him.

Vee and Miri were both in position, and both erecting

similar salt lines. Confident that they were in position I turned back to the lift and poured a line of salt across the threshold to protect the minister.

"I still have no idea how we got here from the depot," the minister hissed. "I know now is a bad time, but if you could explain while you work I'd appreciate it."

"Hassle Aruni." I nodded at the judge, who'd predictably not left his corner of the lift. "I need to arrange our ride."

I tuned back to the rest of the squad, and keyed a missive through my HUD. Several moments later Briff's face filled the holo. "Jer! Are you on the surface?"

"We're up," I explained. "I'm transmitting our coordinates now. We're in pretty deep. Holdout mission, basically. Wights and shamblers are moving in our direction, and sooner or later we're going to get the attention of one of those necromancers. We need to get out of here. Now."

"You got it, Jer," Briff promised. "We'll be there as soon as we can. Rava's a great pilot."

I killed the missive and turned back to our battle lines, or lack of them. Only six of us remained, and only four could fight. Seket stood ready to receive the initial charge, which mostly consisted of wights, as they were faster than the shamblers.

In that instant my gaze passed the wights and the shamblers, until I locked eyes with the pale-skinned necromancer and his pet dragon, the soulshackled Wyrm. They stood well away from the pending battle, quietly observing while making no move to approach or interfere.

He raised a hand then, and offered a friendly wave.

His smile and whole demeanor was all, "hey there, neighbor." It hurt my brain. "Good morning! I hope you slept well. I am genuinely impressed you overcame the Spite. I lost a dram of souls over that one. You're out of spells, though. How will you escape the current predicament? I'm so excited to see how you resolve this."

How do you respond to that? Exhaustion robbed me of any cool, or even mediocre, comebacks. I settled for an eyeroll, raised my pistol, and prepared for battle.

Game time.

I thumbed the ammo selector from spells to my new salt rounds and trotted over to a pile of crates behind Seket's position. It would divide the flow of enemies if he were forced back, and also provided hard cover for my right flank.

The wights rushed toward Seket, but stopped outside the salt line he'd erected. Three sweeps later and his giant sword had eliminated seven wights.

Another wave had already reached him though, and prowled outside the salt line, encircling it as they sought entry.

Behind them a half dozen shamblers had finally shuffled close enough to be a threat, though given how slow they were I suspected Seket wouldn't have any problem dealing with them.

I brought my pistol up and walked it down the line of wights, one after another. Each time a salt round struck, it released a white cloud that detonated inside the spectral form, and the doomed creature's elongated shriek accompanied its dissolution. Just that like all the wights were gone, and I still had one round left.

Damn. I should have made more. A lot more.

Dozens of shamblers were converging on us, with more waves behind them. A pair of necromancers on their strange harnesses pranced behind the ranks, apparently taking the lead from our chatty friend and staying out of it.

"Briff, buddy," I mumbled under my breath. "Now would be a great time for a last minute rescue." There was no sign of the *Remora* on the skyline, no whir of engines, though to be fair there was no atmo either.

Seket's blade was everywhere, and his shield just as lethal a weapon. Both whirred around him, and sliced through any shambler that made it close enough to be a threat. A pair of wights made it to the salt circle, but were still kept at bay for the time being.

I executed one, then switched the selector back to spells, and executed the second with a fire bolt. Again I held my weapon up in disbelief. Wights didn't have any special vulnerability to *fire* like they did *dream*. There was no way a single fire bolt should kill one. But mine had.

Miri finally engaged, and used a pair of life bolts to thin the herd of shamblers before it reached Seket. Good thing, as even the mighty paladin had been taxed to the limit of his abilities.

More shamblers shambled, and more wights clustered. There didn't appear to be an end to them, in any direction I looked.

"My condolences," necromancer buddy called. He'd crept much closer, though still lurked beyond the battle. "You very nearly made it to your ship. Another...two minutes? And you'd actually survive. Pity. I've so enjoyed observing your progress. So inventive. I suppose I will have to locate another candidate."

"We're not dead yet!" I roared back. I used my last few fire bolts to thin the herd, but I knew he was right. We were going to die. There were simply too many. They'd force us back into the lift, where our friend the bone thief would be waiting.

Then I remembered. We had a card that had refused to play itself.

I spun to face Aruni, and my fury made my words sharp and brittle. "You've jerked us around, Aruni. You've asked us to get you to the ship. I've seen your little tricks. I watched you empower Seket, but apparently even that has limits. Whatever magic you've got we need it right now. Either you intervene, or we don't survive long enough for the *Remora* to arrive. Choose, Aruni. You can't stand on the sidelines forever."

The Inuran's shoulders slumped, and a sob centuries in the making rolled out of his gut. His entire body shook for several seconds as he cried. I watched in awkward silence until he mastered himself.

"You're right." Aruni's mouth firmed, and in the blink of an eye his entire body transformed. Majestic wings soared up over his largely human body, more delicate than a hatchlings. Scales small enough to rival grains of sand covered his body, though so fine they resembled pores and could be mistaken for skin. A draconic tail slashed a path in the air behind him, another reminder that he was no human. "The time has come to take an active role. For good or ill I will make my stand, and attempt to rebuild what I can, in the open, though it may be my final death."

Then it hit me. I recognized him. This was one of the two gods who'd been playing Kem'Hedj during the second trial for captain on the *Word of Xal*. The one set ten millennia ago or more.

"Uh, okay." I blinked at him. "I feel like there's some gaps you could fill in right now. Like who you are."

"Later." Aruni strode forward and raised both hands. Each finger released a sea of sigils, and I noted that he drew upon multiple greater paths...to weave a single spell. Nature and artificing came together in a sea of interlocking sigils that swirled over Aruni's head. "I consecrate this place in my name. I am Inura Lifebinder, Inura Bladeforger. I...am the Maker. Unclean things are no longer welcome here."

Vee fell to her knees, and even Seket stopped fighting and turned towards Inura.

I could only sputter. "But...like...is anyone else a god too?" I glanced suspiciously at the minister, and then my companions.

Inura strode forward as his spell competed, and a wave of golden energy rolled out from him. The deck itself shifted to a lighter hue, and the effect rippled outwards in all directions for a hundred meters or more.

Every shambler burst into flame. Every wight was snuffed like a discarded candle. The two nameless necromancers scuttled away in the opposite direction, but failed to outrun the consecration. The divine energy burned them alive, and their harnesses clattered to the deck, the only memory of their existence.

"Oh, my," the chatty necromancer called. "That was unexpected. Necrotis will want to you know you're alive. Neat trick, that. A word of advice if I may, Inura. She's got abandonment issues. Try not to upset her. Maybe bring her a souvenir or something."

The necromancer raised his staff, then slashed the air before him. What he opened resembled a Fissure, but instead of a jagged crack into darkness it was a rip in reality leading to a...paler place. The necromancer stepped inside, and the rip closed in his wake.

A high-pitched whine sounded above me as the *Remora* swept into view, then sailed to a landing not far from where we were sheltering.

"Well, Minister," I panted. "I got you back to the ship."

15

I'd never been so happy to see Briff as when the *Remora*'s landing ramp extended and he offered me a hand up. Kurz helped Vee on the other side, and Miri jumped up unaided, showing off those athletic skills.

I turned around and helped the minister up, noting that her exhaustion might be worse than my own. "We'll get you to some quarters for a nap while we connect with the *Word of Xal*."

"No, I have to—"

"No you don't," I countered. "If you transmit anything from this ship you give away the fact that you're on it. We're hitting orbit nice and quietly, until we can get you to your flagship, or to the *Word of Xal*. I am not taking chances with these guys."

The minister nodded wearily. "You're talking sense."

Vee wrapped an arm around her. "Come with me. I'll help you to some quarters so you can get some rest."

They headed off, which left me staring down the

ramp as we awaited our last arrival. I heaved a relieved sigh when Aruni came around the corner, and not Inura. I knew it was the same person, but I found his Inuran form a lot less intimidating.

"I lived up to my end." I slammed the button next to the ramp and it began to retract into the ship. "How about yours?"

"Captain?" Seket choked out. "I do not believe you should speak to him in such a manner."

I noted that Vee managed a scandalized look over her shoulder before disappearing out of sight with the minister.

"As I mentioned on the moon," Aruni interjected, "you are a paladin a god can be proud of. Thank you."

"I don't mean to press," I pressed, "but you need to come clean, Inura. What kind of game are you playing? Why were you in that courtroom? Why are you following us?"

Inura nodded emotionlessly. "You have honored our accord, and I will do the same. I was on that moon to meet you and Seket. To take your measure. When I made that choice you were still the captain of the *Word of Xal*."

"Oh." I didn't know how I felt about a god taking an interest in me. Another god. "So why all the games? Why not just nuke your way off this planet, and go punch that Great Ship out of the sky? You made it didn't you?"

"Captain," Seket choked, his voice even more scandalized, if that were possible.

"That is no creation of mine. No longer." Inura frowned up at the *Remora*'s hull, and I had the impression he was peering through it. "It has been perverted to necrotech, which devours the souls of the living to power its devices. I snuck aboard and observed the necromancers. They are many and powerful, as you've since seen. I'd hoped to reach you and form a coalition to resist them before it was too late."

"Oops." Totally not sarcasm. "So now what?"

"I don't know," the deity admitted. He sighed and shook his head at me. "I have no special abundance of power. Most of what I was, my ancient body, died during the battle at the Fist of Trakalon. I am not far removed from a mortal archmage in terms of power, and I am nearly as vulnerable to damage. If I earn the wrath of that ship, and they come for me, then I may die the final death."

I lowered my mask and forced calming breaths. So. Tired. "Okay, I'll take this at face value. I'd like to have a further discussion after I've had a chance to sleep. Right now I have bigger concerns. I need to find out what's going on with the *Word of Xal*."

"Wait!" The minister's voice cracked through the hold like thunder. She'd re-emerged into the cargo hold, with Vee tugging at her arm. "You promised to rule in our favor. Was all of that a lie?"

"Of course not." Indignation marred Inura's features. "I am always a silent member of the board of the Consortium. I founded it. I have the authority to issue rulings, and have done so. Your debt is absolved, and the Inurans will trouble your people no more. Though it seems you have greater problems now."

The minister blinked suspiciously at Inura, but Vee

whispered something, and slowly but firmly pulled her from the hold, toward the crew quarters.

"You're welcome to eavesdrop. I'm calling my mother." I issued a missive from my HUD, and turned from Inura as I waited patiently for her to accept. She might be busy running a war room, or asleep, or frantically making repairs. Seconds ticked by.

Finally my mother's face appeared on my HUD. She smiled, though even that little effort piled onto her exhaustion. All of us were in the same sorry state.

"Jerek," she began, eyes searching me as she sought a way to ask the question I knew she desperately wanted to. "Were you able to complete that last assignment?"

"Yeah, it's done." I smiled in a way that I hoped communicated "she's safe." "Can you bring us up to speed? We're just shy of an hour from docking."

"That may not be soon enough." My mother's mouth tightened, and I could tell she was in physical pain. "We think the *Maker's Wrath* will attack, and we don't have enough magic to repel them. If they hit us we're done, unless we can find a massive source of magic."

"How massive?" My shoulders slumped as I began connecting dots, and realized I knew of a massive source.

"The biggest source you can find, child." Visala's face muscled its way into view. "A starship won't do it this time. We need a god. Or a minor Catalyst."

"I hate my job." I closed my eyes.

"Jerek?" There was concern in my mother's voice.

"Well, we have a god," I explained, eyes still closed, "but he's probably not going to be able to help. We'll probably need something stronger. It just so happens that the Inurans have a life reactor powering this part of the moon. Since this place still has power to the lift, I assume it's still running. If we can get that reactor that's probably our best chance."

"Jerek, doing that means not coming back to the ship...." My mother raised a hand to the screen. After a moment her face hardened and she lowered it. "You're right. We need that reactor, unless you really do have a god with you. Do what you can, and keep that last assignment safe so I can read it when you get back."

"Of course." I nodded, then severed the connection in case the necromancers had a way to scry on our connection. "Inura, is there anything that you can do to help them?"

He nodded, though there was a sadness to it. "I've revealed myself. Their leader will soon learn I'm here. If I am not going to flee, then I may as well make a stand on that ship. Be careful, Jerek. You are the best your race has to offer, and I believe a great destiny awaits you."

"That destiny better be the name of a video game, or a hotel where I can get a bed, because I am too tired for any more cryptic god speak." I rose and shuffled off, a shambler in all but name. I figured I could catch a twenty-minute nap before we landed and I had to lead a strike team into the core of a dead planet.

INTERLUDE IV

Necrotis placed a scale on the far edge of the Kem'Hedj board, then stared across the vast chamber, built solely to house this one game. Over the millennia her opponent had become a dear friend. They shared similar backgrounds, and the day would soon come when they met in person. When that happened, though, Necrotis would come as an equal, as she'd proven to be in their centuries long game.

She would bring her own unseen fleet, to rival those already prowling the storming void known as Sanctuary.

A pale slit in the veil opened in the corridor outside her chamber, an affront worthy of note. She withdrew from the game, and approached the corridor, curious at who'd dare to approach in such an impertinent manner.

"Pardon, Mother." Utred knelt on his harness, his staff in full supplicant position. "Before you reap my soul hear my news. Inura has revealed himself on the trade moon. He lives. He consecrated an area to save the boy, and himself. I am positive it is he."

"How?" she thundered. The impossibility endangered all her plans. She'd never have begun had she known the Maker still lived. She'd witnessed memory-scales of his death. How was this possible?

Necrotis smoothed her blouse. She'd simply find out.

As Inura's daughter she understood his magical signature. She knew him as few did. That meant getting a missive through to him, even though he wanted to hide, should be possible.

She moved to the young woman lashed to the matrix, and willed the ship to claim the rest of her. She groaned weakly, once, and then expired quietly.

The scryscreen rippled into a view of a tiny freighter. The very last type of vessel Inura would choose, unless forced to it. Her first clue as to his disposition.

Inura's familiar face stared back at her, the human version of it anyway. The version he'd used to seduce her mother, and countless other women.

"Hello, Father." She inclined her head slightly. "I must admit I am surprised to find you alive. How did you survive the battle at the fist? How did you cloak the possibility of your survival? Even now, it seems, you still know things I do not."

"Daughter?" Inura raised an eyebrow. "You're wearing a mask, but I can tell you that you are no daughter of mine. You murdered my ship. You are the antithesis of everything I stand for."

"I did what you were too weak to," she snarled, her composure shattered. She didn't care. The boy looked on, but he was no longer captain, so she did not bother demanding his removal. "We will finally take vengeance on your wayward children, on the Consortium. What I have done here to this trade moon is merely the beginning. In time I will locate the other two, and they will meet the same fate."

"If you are my daughter," Inura allowed, "then you remember why we outlawed necrotech in the first place, yes? What's changed?"

"Apathy," she answered without hesitation. "I do not care what fate meets this realm. I do, however, care that our enemies and their children die screaming, and as I plan to slaughter them anyway I see no reason not to harvest their bodies and their souls. Waste no material. It was you who taught me that, father."

He cocked his head and studied her, and for a moment the strength of his scrying was incalculable. Her mask thwarted him, somehow, and left him wondering at the face beneath.

"How pathetic that you do not recognize me." She sneered at the once great god. "Though I suppose there's no reason you should. You sired hundreds of us."

At least her father had the good grace to appear embarrassed at that. His ardor had been well known, as had his total lack of attention to a woman as soon as another caught his interest.

"What do you want, Necrotis?" Inura squared his shoulders, though his posture was a brittle thing. A thing she could break easily.

"I want to add the *Word of Xal* to my fleet." She leaned closer to the scry-screen. "If you leave now, then I will allow you to live. I will take that ship, and then I will come for the Inurans. Stay out of my way. Go find a quiet sector on the far side of the galactic core, well away from me. We need never see each other again, and you can find some other race to dupe into worshiping you."

"I cannot allow you to claim that ship." Inura's form shifted, and wings flared behind him. He truly had revealed himself. "I will stop you."

"Will you?" She mused, then offered a coy smile. "I am ready to call your bluff, father. Defend your new little darlings, or I am about to add their souls to my drive."

"Don't do this, whoever you are." Inura's voice rang with desperation, though at least it seemed sincere. "I am a terrible deity, but that doesn't mean you should take it out on the sector. You've gotten your revenge. Take the moon and leave. We will withdraw as well."

"The spirits are whispering, father." A cold, cruel smile cracked her cheeks. "They tell me that the name you used was Aruni. A little on the nose, yes? Aruni? Inura? Your name spelled backwards. You were daring us to find you. You crave oblivion."

"No." Inura shook his head, and she read pity there. "You believe that, but there is power in reflection. A symbiosis greater than the sum of its parts. Xal taught me about that."

"You're telling me that the keys you constructed for the *Spellship* were not merely some flippant joke?" Necrotis paused then, and began to pace. "Perhaps I misjudged you. First you survived, and now you are telling me there is some sort of ritual attached to this naming convention?"

"Not ritual sorcery," her father corrected in that condescending tone he so loved to ooze. "Divine power.

Such pairings are resonant with the universe, and serve as a focal point. Ikadra and Ardaki are forever linked, their names opposite, but their purpose, and power, twin to each other. Together they are far greater than each alone, as is true with all such pairings."

She hated that she'd been wrong about his name. Hated that he still knew depths of magic she'd not yet plumbed.

"I call your bluff, father. It is time to end that ship." She waved a hand and ended the missive, then turned to one of the milky-eyed underlings cabled to the console. "Dispatch our best reaper to take their captain. I want that ship leaderless, in case they somehow survive our assault."

16

We used the trip back to the surface to have a shopping party in the *Remora*'s mess. The forge had plenty of grenade and ammo schematics, including my salt rounds, and when we'd retrieved the ship the reservoirs of materials from the foundry had all been full.

This time I made twelve magazines. The cost was negligible without the crazy Inuran markup, and all of a sudden I could see why they'd stop at nothing to eliminate competitors.

"What are you going to make, Briff?" I stuffed mags into the pouches on both legs. Room was tight as they already bulged with four grenades each. Half were pulse, and half were frag.

Briff gave a noncommittal grunt as he thumbed through schematics, mesmerized by stuff we'd never thought we could afford. I let him be and inspected Rava, who'd already had her turn. A bandolier lined with grenades slashed one side of her chest, and another with magazines crossed the other.

"You're not carrying a spellpistol?" I asked even as I patted mine. I figured she might still be getting used to having spells.

"Nah." She shook her head. "I don't really understand it well enough to use it yet. I trust tech. I'm going to stick to what I know. I'll take the magical strength buff though. That part of *fire* is pretty cool."

"Captain," Seket called from the doorway. He still wore his golden armor, sans the helmet. "I'm out of spells, and my armor is heavily damaged. I will accompany you back to the core, but even with the Maker's blessing I'm not sure how much use I'll be."

"You've done enough." I nodded. "I've got another job for you in any case. The minister is staying here, and I need someone to fly the ship. Stand by to lift off. As soon as Vee gives us a course I'll pass it along."

"Thank you, Captain." Seket saluted with fist over heart, then trotted off toward the bridge.

"You want me to do what now?" Vee's head came up from where it had been resting against a bulkhead, and her eyes opened. She still clutched a pile of grenades in her lap, like a child might a doll while sleeping.

"Here's my thinking," I explained, praying that my idea made sense. "The cores are going to be difficult to reach, but they must be close to the areas where they operate. The longer the conduit, the more runes have to be maintained. The cannon is probably connected to one of the cores, and I bet if we can get in that barrel, then we can find a maintenance hatch or something that will lead directly to it. That's where you come in. We need to figure out where the cores are, and how to get there."

"Hmm." Vee twirled the end of her ponytail around one finger as she considered that. "That sort of information isn't going to be public. Miri, do you know anything about the cores that we don't?"

Miri had fallen asleep against a bulkhead, her mouth open and emitting faint snores. At the sound of her name the PSA lurched awake and blinked at Vee. "Hmm? You need fashion advice? Finally."

"Miri," Vee repeated patiently, though a vein throbbed near her temple. "Do you know anything about how to reach the cores that power the cannon?"

"I know that maintenance crews work it daily. Dozens of maintenance crews." She rose with a stretch, suddenly full of energy like a toddler after a nap. Maybe Inurans needed less sleep. "If we want to reach a core, those areas will be flagged as restricted. We might have to blow open a few doors, but it looks like we're not hurting for explosives."

"No," Briff confirmed, "but it does look like we're running out of raw materials for non-organic schematics. Plastics, metals, several types of magic, and a few other materials I don't recognize are at critical levels."

"We'll deal with that once we get back. Has anyone seen the minister?" I inspected the crack down my HUD, and noted that it was smaller than it had been. I hoped a lot more time passed before I got shot again.

"She's asleep." Vee rolled her neck, then donned her helmet. "I gave her a sedative. She should sleep until morning...no matter what happens."

I appreciated the gesture, especially from Vee who came from a culture that favored pragmatism over mercy or sentiment. If it came to the worst and wights got on the ship she wouldn't feel a thing.

"Briff, you're on point until we reach the core, then you're in charge of carrying the thing back." I nodded at Rava next. "You're floating. Be where you can do the most damage, but focus on keeping them off our backs. Vee, I know you're running close to dry. Stay out of combat if you can. We need you to disconnect the core when we reach it. Miri, you've lived up to your end of the deal. We'd love to have you along, but if you want to stay with the ship I'll pay you for the run and we can call it there."

Miri planted a shapely leg on a cargo drum and slammed a magazine home in her spellpistol, one of the fancy Mk VII's that could fire both conventional rounds and spells. "If you were serious about having me in the crew? I'm in it until we're done. Lurker girl needs someone looking out for her on this op. Let's make that me, so you can do your job. I keep her safe, and you can focus."

"We'd love to have you." I nodded at Rava. "Miri, meet my sister, Rava. Rava, this is Miri. She's a personal shopping assistant, and right now I need to acquire a *life* core."

"Your sister?" Miri offered hand to Rava, who shook it firmly. "Guess I want to stay on her good side. You keep me alive, and we're going to be great friends. I'll take you shopping."

"Great. Show me something badass in leather. Shall we?" Rava nodded at the ramp, which had begun to descend.

Vee glowered after them both, of course. I couldn't blame her.

It meant the sector to me that they were bantering when I knew damned well everyone had passed exhaustion hours ago. We weren't just out of spells. We were physically pushing our limits. Rava and Briff were more fresh, but not that much more. We'd be relying heavily on them.

"Wait, where's Kurz?" I spun around and realized I hadn't seen him since I'd re-boarded.

"Still asleep." Briff shrugged, and his wings pressed up against his back in what I'd come to know as what-did-briff-do. "Should I have woken him?"

"No, you did great." I mentally calculated how long it would take us to reach the cannon. "Go ahead and wake him now though. Tell him to be ready in five. We're going to want everything he can bring to the table. Tell him to bring his best stuff."

And by stuff I meant souls. That was easier for me to accept before I'd become aware of these necromancers. I still didn't even know what they called themselves. Necros? Whoever they were, they'd made terrible house guests on the trade moon so far.

There I went again trying to ignore my guilt about Kurz. He wasn't a necromancer in the sense that he didn't practice the greater path of binding souls, but he did see them as a power source. And, now that it had become clear that the *Inura's Grace* had been a sham, I wondered if the soulcatchers had been nothing but dupes serving the necromancers. A way to bring victims in.

If it came down to the last O_2 tank, would Kurz fight

with us? I wanted to think so, but that wasn't something I could afford to just take for granted.

"Jerek!" Vee wore one of those smiles that made me look right past Miri without a second glance. "I've found the right access port, I think. Work orders are in a public Quantum database. We can enter a maintenance hatch, and it's a short crawl into the main chamber. From there we follow the cables straight to the core."

"That sounds way too simple." I shook my head. "I'm not buying it. There's going to be crazy buzzsaw droids, or undead exes, or something else that will suck to deal with."

"Well I know where to go at least." Her smiled faded a tick. "I'll upload the coordinates to Seket."

"Standing by," Seket's voice crackled over the comm. I hadn't even seen him leave the cargo hold. Or had I? I couldn't remember any more. Should I take some stims? No, that seemed like a bad idea. I couldn't afford to crash in the middle of fleeing with the core.

The ship's drive rumbled to life, and I patched my HUD into external sensors so I could see as we whipped around the trade moon. The cannon's barrel needed some sort of word beyond gargantuan, and suggested the moon was compensating for something. Maybe it had wanted to be a planet.

We flew directly down the barrel. All the way down. The ship dropped lower and lower as the chrome walls whipped by. There was no chance the cannon would fire, but I still closed my eyes and prayed to the Maker. I promptly stopped when I realized Inura might actually hear that prayer. Awkward. I was used to the Maker being an abstract, not an underpowered navel-gazing has-been.

The *Remora* slowed outside a three-meter circular corridor leading to thick door with a panel strapped to the outside. "Let's move out, people. We have work to do."

An awful buzz came from above, and a dozen attack drones hummed toward the *Remora*. Each carried a plasma cannon, and they fired almost as one, a stream of star-stuff, the conventional kind, slamming into the aft side in a shower of debris that tore past the wards and left deep furrows in the hull.

"Go! GO!" I roared.

17

The drones swarmed around the *Remora*, but wards quickly sprang up around the freighter, blunting their assault. Seket could handle it.

I turned back to the console where Vee crouched, and stifled the urge to peer over her shoulder and offer advice. Exhaustion pulsed in me like a living thing, but on the plus side, I'd passed the point where my body wanted sleep.

Now I just wanted to curl up somewhere and drool. No, strike that. Just curl up. Drooling sounded like a lot of effort.

BEEP! The console chimed, and the thick black door slid into the wall like an iris exposing the pupil of a dark god.

No one spoke. We all knew our jobs. Rava trotted in first, closely followed by Miri. Kurz surprised me by going next. I hung back with Vee, and didn't need to glance behind me to know that Briff would be bringing up the rear.

Seket was amazing, but I vastly preferred having the hatchling watching my back. Briff and I had been a team for almost five years now, and friends long before that. I'd barely come up to his waist when we'd first met.

Most of the kids had been afraid of him, but I really enjoyed hanging out because long after the other kids started getting into sports or holo games, we were still playing make believe with dice and a few battered *Spell-casting & Starships* books.

I'd die for that scaly bundle of teeth, no questions.

We advanced up a narrow corridor, which spilled into a room filled with treasure and happiness. I'm lying. It was FUBAR, ancient Terran for screwed, though we can't trace the origin of the word.

A long cable about three meters thick extended from just beneath us out into a vast gulf of empty space. When I say vast...the interior of the planet was partially hollow and I could see for hundreds of kilometers.

Our cable snaked out to one of many free-floating structures, with a pair of maintenance doors and no other sign of entry. Flocks of drones swirled through the vast cavern, but none seemed to have noted our arrival.

"Be careful," Vee called as she took point on the cable. "This thing is pretty stable, but it will start to sway if we're all on it at the same time. Keep maybe ten meters between each of us, and don't walk too quickly. Especially you, Briff."

"Okay." His wings sagged.

"It's just that you're carrying a spellcannon," Vee pointed out, though it didn't seem to help. She gave a shrug, and started up the cable.

Rava came next, then Miri. I waited until a gap opened, then trotted onto the cable. Could I summon enough *void* to make the armor fly if I toppled off? I honestly didn't know. My kingdom for some mana beer and a cot.

The cable's slow sway didn't deter me, and I picked a careful path, though I did hesitate when Briff stepped onto the cable behind me. The swaying worsened, and I flung my arms out for stability.

My eyes focused on the next step as I picked a path forward, and tried not to worry about what might go wrong. I couldn't really control it. I could only get through it as quickly and efficiently as possible.

Several tense minutes later the cable began sloping upward again, indicating that we'd passed the midway point. We'd all found a rhythm now, and the swaying seemed manageable. Enough that I risked a few glances around us.

The closest swarm of drones lay so distant I couldn't make out more than specks. Presumably they had orders, or a patrol route, and were unlikely to meddle with something this far away.

A glance at our route showed Vee reaching the structure housing the core. Now that we were closer I could see its muted blaze through the polarized windows on the structure. More than that I could feel the power of it, the majesty. We were seeing the essence of the universe, a primal magic that transcended any singular god. Pure *life*...harnessed to power this moon.

"This is amazing." Vee pressed her hands up against the window. "It will take me a few minutes to hack the door, then a few more to disconnect the core. We need to be careful. If I make a mistake and the casing cracks? All of us are probably vaporized, though we'll die knowing we're freeing the Maker's essence."

I hadn't asked her where she stood on the whole Inura/Aruni thing. I didn't really know where I stood, and my faith wasn't invested in the outcome like hers was.

"We trust you, Vee. Everyone else, keep down and alert us if you see something headed our way."

I took my own advice, and crept to the far side of the structure. It wasn't that I didn't badly want to inspect the Inuran tech. I did. But I also wanted to live, and I needed to do my job and let Vee do hers. It sucked not getting to do the fun stuff anymore.

When we were done maybe I could look into turning in my adulting membership card. Probably not.

"Contact," I whispered into the comms.

A swarm of drones were moving on a zigzag course that would take them alarmingly close to our platform.

I reached into my pocket, and fished out a magazine of explosive rounds. I only had two, because I'd stocked up on salt rounds. Brilliant. How the depths did I keep bringing the wrong ammo? This is why I prefer spells.

The magazine slammed home, and I brought the pistol up in time to sight down the barrel at the lead drone. I stroked the trigger, and it kicked violently, as a high velocity hunk of explosive love slammed into the drone's central casing.

Imagine my surprise when the drone just exploded. No muss. No fuss. That thing just shattered.

"Nice shot," Rava called with a grin. "Maybe you can

teach me how to shoot later." She raised her assault rifle, and snapped off a pair of shots with no apparent aim, though I knew cyberware provided her with more telemetry than I'd ever have.

The next two drones exploded in quick succession.

Miri raised her pistol, and offed the next two as if keeping score, though she didn't say it aloud. Her smirk said all she didn't.

A sharp high-pitched hum came from behind me, and Briff's spellcannon kicked. I'd forgotten he still had magic, since he'd been on the ship.

A ball of pure plasma sailed into one drone with so much force it knocked the doomed robot into a companion, which also detonated.

But more drones came. We kept firing, and they kept coming. Eventually one got close enough to fire a plasma cannon at Briff. He set his feet and tail against the deck, and encircled himself with his heavily-armored wings.

The plasma slammed into him, and he slid back several paces, but kept his footing. His wings flared outward, and he lobbed another plasma ball at the offending drone. Scratch other robot.

Then, just like that, the flow ended. We stood there panting, eyeing each other in disbelief. We'd survived, and taken very little damage.

"More will be coming," Miri promised. "They'll transmit our location, and identify us as a threat. We need to work quickly, or they may send something really nasty to dissuade us. The Consortium does not play nicely, trust me."

Vee still knelt next to the panel, though she'd found a

way to get it open, and had exposed a variety of runes, which she was now tinkering with.

"I don't want to rush you, Vee," I nagged like a man who fears giant robots, or whatever the Inurans sent. "We need to be out of here in the next three minutes."

"That's not possible," she countered. "Figure out a way to hold this platform, because I need more time."

My shoulders sank. This had officially become the worst day on the job ever. I forced iron right back into my posture, and my shoulders came up as I faced my team.

"You heard the lady. Get into the best position you can to watch this door." I set my back next to the panel where Vee sat tinkering. "Nothing gets past us. Nothing.

18

The first two minutes or so were great. No Inuran response came, though all of us knew it would.

Near the end of the second minute Vee gave a triumphant cry, and the door opened. She darted inside to work her magic on the core itself, and I kept watch for trouble.

It came swiftly.

Something twinkled in the distance, and grew larger as it flew in our direction. It passed a cloud of drones, which lent it perspective, and I realized that thing had to be ten or twelve meters tall. It had arms and legs, and a pair of wings...like a giant mechanical hatchling, but more humanoid.

More importantly it carried an appropriately over-sized spellrifle, and I really didn't want to be on the receiving end of it.

"Contact!" I hissed into the comm. "Form up on me.

Vee, keep doing your thing. Everyone else, I need a dead mech. Kill that thing."

"Captain, I do not see how we can inflict any meaningful damage." Kurz's statement came as flat facts. "Its resistance will block all spells, and only Briff and I have those, in any case. And your explosive rounds will not be effective."

"All that's probably true, but we need to find a weakness if it exists. Think about how to use your resources creatively. What can your souls do?" Dammit, I hated situations like this. "Spread out. Do what we can to distract it until we can figure out a way to stop it. See if we can hit the head with grenades to damage the sensors. Use the structure for cover."

I hoped its reluctance to damage the core's storage unit would prevent it from attacking us.

"I've got a shot." Rava dropped to one knee and snapped her rifle to her shoulder. She tracked for several seconds, then the rifle roared and her shoulder jerked back.

One of the two antennae on the mech's head detonated, and the knight winced, then twisted to bring an arm up and deflect Rava's next shot.

Miri hefted a grenade, and when the warrior had closed, lunged from cover long enough to lob it toward the mech. Her aim was good, and it exploded against the shoulder, showering the face with shrapnel. Unfortunately, the second antenna survived, as did the optics. This thing was damned tough.

The mecha knight delivered a vicious kick that Miri ducked by falling back around a corner of the building. It twisted one hand and fired the spellrifle at Briff. The shot knocked the hatchling off the platform, and he tumbled into the abyss, toward the gravity well that would suck him into whatever lay at the center of the planet.

"Nooo!" I roared. Rage burned away the exhaustion, and I charged the mecha, which stood on the far side of the platform. I knew my pistol wouldn't do squat, so I holstered it, then leapt onto the mech's leg.

An arm whooshed over my head as I clambered up to the thigh, then maneuvered around the back as it struggled in vain to reach me.

"Keep it busy, Jer!" Briff roared from behind. I risked a look, and spotted him hovering, his wings flapping hard behind him. He landed on the cable, and his spellcannon bucked.

A fat ball of plasma slammed into the mech's chest, and cracks spread across the armor for several meters.

"Come get some, uh, mech...thing." Briff lobbed another plasma ball, but the thing dodged out of the way this time.

Which meant it wasn't paying attention to me.

I clambered up further, and nestled myself behind the head. The antenna lay within reach so I grabbed it, and swung around the mech's face. My free hand shot out and I planted it against the right eye. "Weaken."

Nara's magic flowed through me, and the no doubt nearly indestructible crystal became destructible. I yanked my pistol out and shot it with an explosive round, and the eye shattered.

Have I mentioned I can be petty? I wrenched the antenna loose, effectively blinding the sensors. This thing was one optic away from total blindness, and that was exactly what...uh oh.

My hero moment ended when the mech got a hand around both of my legs. The massive mechanical fingers tightened, and my paper doll flared red as my legs were crushed together and the internal alarms began full panic mode.

The mech lurched as one of Miri's grenades exploded violently beneath its feet. The stumble loosened its grip, and I wiggled free and onto the back where neither arm could reach me. Thank the depths my armor was tough, or both my legs would have been broken.

I couldn't afford to let it get ahead of me again.

The mech brought up its rifle, and hip shot at Briff. The aim was true, and knocked the hatchling back along the cable. His spellcannon tumbled over the side, and one of his wings had all the scaled webbing burned away until nothing but skeleton remained.

Briff screeched, and pulled the ruined wing close against his body as he clung to the cable. If he fell off again there would be no flying. We needed to stop this thing. Now.

I glanced at Vee, and she'd disconnected most of the cables connecting the core to the rune matrix housing.

"Captain!" Kurz roared. My attention shifted his way in time to see him lob a green vial at me.

I caught it instinctively, and inspected the contents. Hellish green smoke swirled within, and as I watched, a pair of eyes peered hatefully out at me.

"Slam the soul into the mech's eye. The soul will consume all nearby magic until it explodes."

Explodes. I was, quite literally, using a soul as a bomb. That asked some troubling questions that I shoved down into the recesses to leave me free to fight. Guilt, if warranted, could come later.

I surged to my feet, and nearly toppled off the mech, but caught myself against the shoulder. The head swiveled in my direction, and I realized in that terrible moment that my survival, my friends' survival, might come down to my athleticism.

We were doomed.

I lobbed the green vial toward the broken eye like a ball sailing toward a lifewine jug back at festival. I'd been terrible at that game, and pro-tip...don't try to impress a date if you're bad at hitting lifewine jugs, like I was.

Fate, the universe, and maybe my dad's ghost guided the throw, and it sailed into the empty eye socket. The vial cracked, and greenish smoke exploded outward to fill the socket.

One of the mech's hands shot up to its face to cover the wound, and I realized that I'd been thinking of this thing as a machine. It wasn't. This was an elidmagus, and that meant it was alive.

The mech thrashed in pain as the soul did its work, but I didn't stick around to watch. I dove from the shoulder, and rolled with the fall. Sparks skittered across the platform as I tumbled across it, but I flipped over and directed my tumble onto the cable, where I recovered and somehow found my footing.

I wish I'd recorded that.

"Briff, you okay?" I sprinted over to my friend, who

had risen to his feet, but had an arm wrapped around his wounded wing.

"Yeah," he croaked. "Vee can heal it after we get back to the ship. Did...did we win?" He gawked at something behind him, and I spun to see what had become of the mech.

The creature had fallen to its knees on the far corner of the platform, and now clutched its head with both arms. A high-pitched whine grew from inside the head, and a moment later the head, the mech's hands, and shoulders were consumed in a magical explosion.

I sank to my knees on the cable, and ordered my mask to slither off my face so I could catch my breath. Sweat coated me. "Miri, how much time did that buy us?"

"Not much," she called back. She gave a low whistle. "I'm impressed. Your team took down an Inuran Mark IX assault mech."

"Our team," Kurz corrected. "You were instrumental with the well placed grenade. The captain clearly chose well when selecting you as a new crew member, though if you continue to antagonize my sister you will wake up in an airlock."

Miri and I just blinked at the soulcatcher, whose monotone voice hadn't changed a bit from the compliment to the threat.

"I've done it!" Vee's triumphant cry came from inside the structure. "Get Briff in here. There's no way I can carry this. I just need to withdraw this last cable, and—"

The blazing energy in the core ceased for a moment, and the loss of power rippled outward to each of the dozen cables connected to the platform. The circuitry darkened, and the wave of blackness swept outwards to every area their theft had suddenly deprived of power. Kilometers of lights darkened.

"I feel like that's going to get a response." Miri gave me a half grin. "Maybe run?"

"Briff, how do you feel about carrying a magical star in a box?"

"I'm green, Jer." His good wing rose majestically over him.

"That's why I love you, bud." I clapped him on his good side, and moved out of the way so he could get access to the core.

The darkness continued to spread, which didn't alarm me. Then one of the cables popped off the platform, and swung out over the abyss before it began retracting into the wall.

"Oh, shit," I roared. "It's going into some sort of stasis mode. Get onto the cable, and secure yourselves. Now!"

19

"Go, now!" I hustled Miri toward the cable, and Rava leapt over her and drove her spurs into the dense rubber. Ours hadn't disconnected yet, but every three seconds another did, and we were only a few down the line. "Briff, buddy, let's do this."

"I'm on it, Jer!" Briff squatted down, and hefted the reactor with a tremendous groan. "It's pretty heavy, but I got this."

He lumbered out of the structure, and as he passed Vee she extended a bracelet and a wave of golden energy rushed into his wounded wing. Scales and leathery membrane regrew, partially at least. "Sorry, that's all I had left."

"Thanks, Vee," Briff grunted as he stepped onto the cable. "I should be able to—". His tail slammed spike first into the cable, and sank all the way in. "There we go."

"Everyone hang on!" I yelled as the last cable before ours popped off the platform.

Ours came a moment later, and we were in free fall for several seconds.

The vertigo passed when the cable began retracting into the wall, and carrying us upwards with it. The cable retracted swiftly, but not so swiftly that I worried. We should have been able to jump off at the top, though if anyone messed up they'd likely plummet to their death. No pressure.

I tightened my grip on the corded bands that ran every ten or so meters, and held on until we reached the receptacle where the cable gathered. Above us lights were clicking off, making the jump trickier as darkness overtook the ledge above us.

"Time your releases, people," I barked into the comm in exactly the way I imagined my father would have. "This is routine." Even though I knew it to be anything but.

Miri made the jump first, and made it look easy. Rava jumped higher, and landed further up along the ledge, just to show she could.

Next came Briff, and that was the part where I held my breath. He carried so much weight, and he was still wounded.

Briff didn't care. He flung himself upwards with a kick from both legs and the tail. He swung up over the edge with a meter to spare, and rolled until he hit the wall, the reactor still cradled against his chest.

Then it was Vee's turn, and she rolled over without trouble.

When mine got there I focused, and flung myself up

over the edge. Vee caught my hand, and helped me to my feet.

"Nice work, everyone!"

All the light in our section abruptly vanished as the power drain reached this section.

"Crap. Vee, see if we can retrace our steps." I nodded at the black metal iris we'd come through earlier, which was closed again. "Can you get that thing open?"

"I don't understand why we don't see a response squad coming our way." Miri nudged me to get my attention. "Look. There are no drones anywhere. They've all cleared out."

"Something must be a bigger target than us," I reasoned, even as my eyes found the cause. The walkway we stood on ringed this entire massive planetary space, and might be thousands of kilometers long.

About two kilometers distant a female necromancer and her horde of minions were overcoming a wave of drones. Specks of black streaked down from above, and I enhanced my vision for a better look. "They're some sort of bats, I think. And they're wrecking drones...and she's looking this way. Uh...she's looking at me."

The necromancer waved her staff furiously in my direction, and the cloud of bats started our way.

"Vee, can you get that iris open?" I drew my pistol again. "We're not going to be able to hold them for long, if at all."

Vee didn't answer immediately, and instead knelt next to the panel. After a moment she turned in my direction, gaze bereft of hope. "There's no power. The door is dead.

I'm sorry, Jerek. I should have considered what would happen when we removed the core."

"That's on all of us. Any one of us could have thought of it." I turned back to the approaching flock of dead bats. "Let's do what damage we can. Vee, if you have any ideas, I'm open to them. Can you use the core somehow?"

"Uhh." She seemed reluctant to answer.

I turned back and saw the agony on her face. "I can crack the casing. If I get it right, and it's a small crack, it will roast any unliving, demons, or dream wraiths that get close. If I get it wrong...well, we could trigger a chain reaction that causes the other cores to detonate. It would destroy the moon and anything orbiting it."

The knowledge hit me like explosive decompression.

"If we triggered that chain reaction intentionally are you certain it would destroy the moon?" My hands began to shake as the ramifications of my plan became clear.

"Blowing it up would make us fugitives, if we lived. And there could still be survivors," Miri pointed out. "If we do this we're dooming anyone who might still make it off. Other survivors, like us."

"They're doomed anyway." Kurz's flat tone made it clear this was a calculation to him. "If we do this we ensure that this place doesn't become a factory for our enemies. If we do not deprive them of this place, then what is to stop these necromancers from retrofitting it into a necrotech moon?"

"You both make good points." I glanced at the approaching bats. They'd be on us soon. "Those transports dropped the necromancers off here for a reason. They're here to corral the unliving, but what then? Retrofitting this place is the next logical step, and then they have a Great Ship *and* a trade moon. If we have a chance to stop that...I know it's callous, but I say we do it. Even if it means our lives."

"I'm not even sure cracking the casing will blow up the moon," Vee pointed out. She massaged the back of her neck as she inspected the casing. "What do you want me to do?"

"Best case we deprive our enemies this place. Worst case we kill some bats. Crack the casing." I turned back to the flock of bats. They were close enough that I could see their fangs and claws, and the wicked barb on their tails. The same hellish green light lived in their eyes as they swarmed closer.

"Maker, forgive me." Vee raised her bracelet, and touched it to a clasp along the top of the containment unit. It popped open, and she repeated the gesture seven more times in quick succession.

I very nearly forgot to swap ammo, but at the last second remembered I had salt rounds, and swapped back from explosive. I took hasty aim and began squeezing off rounds at the approaching swarm. Due to the density of the swarm, each shot killed at least one bat, and some destroyed two.

But there were a lot of bats.

The swarm crashed over us, and my HUD went red as claws and tails stabbed into my amor. A spike crashed through the faceplate directly over my eye, and the HUD went dark, leaving me with a needle millimeters from my eye.

I activated my sight, and shot the thing in the face

with a salt round. The creature's body slumped as a sickly black-green cloud dissipated over it.

Another spike bit through my armor and into my calf, and I screamed as poker-hot pain commanded my attention.

More wounds flared as they swarmed over us, and I had just enough time to wonder what I could have done better...and then the core exploded.

Brilliant magic washed over us, and I hoped that I'd at least get to go on some sort of magical trip before the torrent of divinity incinerated my frail mortal body. At least it would wipe out the unliving, and that necromancer, even if I wasn't here to see it happen.

Ah, spite...enjoyable when it was the last thing I had left.

20

I t turned out I got my wish. There was a magical trip before the end. As the golden brilliance washed over me my understanding of the universe leapt. Connections linked everything together.

Energy. Matter. Thought. Magic. Time. All of it was part of a singular whole. A system. A cycle. A Great Cycle.

As the magic permeated me I glimpsed a tremendous galaxy-sized purple star. It pulsed out wave after wave of chaotic magic, and each pulse grew and changed into a dizzying array of souls.

These souls swam through the chaos, and founded ephemeral kingdoms, and died in *dream* storms or found their end in other ways.

These souls were not lost, and instead passed to a new realm. A realm of *life*. Our realm.

The erstwhile souls remembered little, in most cases, but their essence was preserved in new bodies. New lives. Time continued to spin enterally, and each of these lives ended.

Their souls passed to the next realm, the spirit realm. From the moment of their entry their essence drained into a negative sun at the center of the realm.

My new understanding told me this negative sun was also the blazing purple sun. They were one and the same.

Was I observing the structure of the universe?

"Yes." To my immense shock a ghostly version of Inura hovered near me. "You are witnessing the Great Cycle, as only an elder god can. The vision will fade quickly, though your memory of the structure will scar you forever."

"I didn't see the Umbral Depths." I tried to focus the Cycle, but gave up and let the vision take me where it would.

"The Depths lie outside the cycle, which is why they are so convenient for travel." Inura folded his arms and raised a patch of platinum scales meant to mimic an eyebrow. "You haven't asked how I've come to be here."

"Seems pretty obvious." It was my turn to raise an eyebrow. "You're a literal god. You've been scrying on me, and when you saw me get into trouble you intervened, right?"

"Perhaps." Inura shrugged, more than a little petulantly. "I warded the lot of you from the blunt of the blast, but only enough to spare your lives. As a result of my intervention you've been blessed with a large reservoir of *life* magic. All of you. And see the results of your efforts."

The vision dissolved and I was back outside the Iris. I rose slowly to my feet, the ghostly vision of Inura still there.

The bats were gone. The necromancer was gone. So

were the drones and every platform, I realized. The cavern had been effectively hollowed out, though enough lights remained to see by. Barely.

"So much for destroying the moon." I clenched a fist. "We wasted the core, and didn't even dent it."

"Not so." Inura offered a tentative smile. "You robbed the moon of power, and destroyed any chance of this monstrosity ever being mobile. Effectively it is as inert as a real moon. Stationary. The necromancers can still harvest the souls, and some of the tech, but the ships got off, and you burnt out the most valuable thing remaining. They're trapped."

"True, but it doesn't feel like a win." I shook my head, too exhausted to care that I'd once again disagreed with a god. "This place makes an excellent staging area to take the other Great Ships. For all we know Necrotis has already been retrofitting one or more of them with necrotech like she did the *Maker's Wrath*."

"Perhaps," Inura allowed with another shrug. "Your friends are waking. Your new magic should make escape a trivial thing."

"What about the core?" I raced to its side to see if I could determine how much magic remained within it. I couldn't go back to the *Word* empty handed.

The readout on the side read 12%. That wan't zero, at least, though I had no idea how much would survive the conversion if I fed this thing to the *Word*. Enough. It had to be.

Vee clambered to her feet first, though Rava wasn't far behind. Kurz rose with a groan and a stretch, while Miri slumbered blissfully on. It was Briff I focused on though.

The hatchling's wing had grown back entirely, and his scales had lightened in hue to a polished white. His eyes fluttered open. "Jer?"

"How ya feelin', bud?" I offered him a hand, though of course I was far too light to help him to his feet.

"Good. Great even." He stood up and stretched. "Like I had the best night sleep."

I stifled the immediate envy. It had been exactly seventy-eight years since I'd last slept.

"Can you grab that core? We still need to get out of here."

"Yeah." Briff trotted over and picked the core up with almost no effort this time. "It's a lot lighter for some reason."

"Most of the power is gone. Guess it had mass, like plasma." I moved to join Vee, who stared down at the golden glow from both hands in wonder. "We all got hit with a blast of *life* magic. You saved our asses, and gave us a Catalyzation."

A blazing hunk of green-gold *life* throbbed in my chest, strong and clear, and...very much opposite of *void*. My study of the magic ended when an insistent voice overpowered everything.

Name. My pistol's voice rang in my head, I knew instinctively that it came from the weapon. *Need. Name!*

"Uh." She'd kind of put me on the spot. "Ariela...two?"

No! New name. Pretty name. Deadly name.

"That's a tall order," I muttered, aware that only I could hear the pistol. At least they could see Inura...I hoped. I did not need that many disembodied voices in my head. Had my armor Catalyzed as well? If so, would it start talking too? "Vee, what was your mother's name?"

"Dez," Vee replied, though I'm not certain she was even aware I was there. Her hands had begun to glow brightly, and I noted that her bracelet had grown. Tiny white sigils now ringed the edge, and I wished I had the time to study them.

"All right, pistol," I decided aloud. "How about Dez? It's beautiful, like Vee, and new, and...uh...deadly." I had no idea what made a name deadly, but technically Dez had just been born so maybe she didn't either.

"Wait." Rava nudged my shoulder with her fist. "Jer, if we all got *life* magic how come I can't feel it? That actually seems useful. I want to test it out."

I did a double take when I glanced at Rava. "Oh, no."

"What?" Rava's now perfect eyes widened.

Inura's specter began to chuckle.

"*Life* can express itself in a few ways." I struggled for a way to break it gently. "I received *life* magic...you, ah, became more attractive?"

"Are you kidding me?" Rava thundered, death lurking in those eyes. "I lost the chance at healing magic so I can...be pretty?"

"Beauty," Inura interjected, "is resonant with *life*. Symmetry. Balance. In mind and in form."

"Doesn't seem very balanced to me." Rava stalked off toward the iris, and delivered a strong kick. "And it doesn't seem like we're getting this open."

"I must return to the *Word*. Battle commences. Return swiftly, young Jerek." Inura offered a low bow that included his wings and tail.

"Keep them alive if you can," I pleaded, but he was already gone. I allowed myself a single calming breath, and then I kept on as if this was all part of the plan. "Vee, what's the news on the iris?"

She shook her head. "It isn't opening. We need another way out."

"A lift maybe?" Miri stifled a yawn. I didn't see when she'd woken, but she was on her feet now. "Or we try to blast through that thing?"

"I counted three more on the way in." I shook my head. "We're not going to brute force it. If I had *void* we could blink past them. Vee, can you find me a maintenance lift near here? And, if you can, can we use the remaining *life* in the core to power it?"

"I can rig something up pretty quickly." She brightened and offered the first smile I'd seen in a while. "My magic...it's stronger now, Jerek. My connection to the Maker is deeper."

"I finally named the pistol you built." I dodged the Inura conundrum by changing the subject. It wasn't that I didn't want to share her joy, but more and more it appeared the Maker wasn't who she thought he was. "Her name is Dez. She chose it."

Vee's eyes began to water. It must have been the, ah, O_2 scrubbers. She cleared her throat. "I'll find us a lift. We should get moving." She started following the wall to the right, and we trailed after her, as far from the edge of the walkway as possible.

Why hadn't they installed a railing? Maybe maintenance people were cheaper than railings. Vee trotted along for a good six hundred meters or so before making a sharp right up one of the corridors we'd passed.

It led to a pair of small lifts, each able to hold four people or one Briff. Neither appeared to have power, which we'd expected, of course.

Vee raised a hand and her bracelet flared. A river of white sigils swam from her palm to the core, then emerged as a thick double helix, rich with *life* magic. It flowed toward the panel outside the lift, and the river of sigils disappeared Inside.

The lift flared to life.

"Girls who save my ass are so hot." Exhaustion had disabled whatever filter remained, and I winced, but to my surprise both Miri and Vee laughed at my joke. I'd been funny.

Damn, I wish I'd recorded that too.

I closed my eyes and waited for the doors to open. Someday I would get to lay down.

INTERLUDE V

Visala hated her role in this farce, hated the powerlessness of it. She hated that no other Wyrms existed to share the burden, only half-trained children still grieving the loss of their world.

In a way, the *Maker's Wrath* was a blessing in that it afforded common cause. Children scurried in their assigned squads, securing all routes in and out of the hangar with expanding salt rings, each ten meters from the last.

It would slow advancing spirits, and give the defenders time to use their considerable magical power. Half-trained mages, perhaps, but mages still.

Time and space swirled around her suddenly as a teleport seized her. Visala appeared on the *Word*'s bridge, a couple meters from the new captain, who she still thought of as the boy's mother, or the sub, if thinking about her role at the academy during the time Visala had spent looking for her grandfather.

She'd returned after the Battle of the Fist, when there

was no longer a point. Inura had been disintegrated by Xal'Aran, the demonic spawn of Xal. She'd have her revenge, some day, but for now her Outriders mattered more. These children needed her. Maker knew this woman wasn't going to watch out for them.

"I'm sorry for plucking you from whatever you were doing." Captain Irala nodded at the scry-screen, which displayed the *Maker's Wrath*.

Their enemy's main cannon filled with a spectral glow, the same glow that had heralded the destruction of the trade moon.

"Are your students in place?" Irala demanded.

"The matrices are staffed." Irala clenched annoyingly human fists. "The children are not ready. There will be casualties."

The captain didn't reply to that. Visala had encountered that kind of end-justifies-the-means thinking many times. That's how you got necromancers claiming to avenge a god sworn to stop necromancy.

"It's happening." A river of unclean souls swam from the enemy vessel, and crashed over their ship in a terrifying tide.

The *Word* rumbled as the wards struggled to repulse the beam, but on and on it went, more and more souls poured into the crumbling wards, distending them until they snapped.

Wights and angers and spites and worse swam through the gaps, infesting parts of the ship. Finally the beam ceased, and the enemy cannon gave a satisfied rumble before going dark.

"Guardian, status report on the mages in the backup

matrices?" The captain kept her composure, though Visala noted the tremor in the woman's hands. She was strong; even Visala had to give her that.

The holographic hatchling appeared before the captain. "Seven mages were consumed entirely. Nine more had their magical ability burned out. They are mages no longer."

The captain refused to look at Visala when she spoke. "Do you have another group of volunteers ready to go?"

"We do," Visala confirmed. "They'll keep dying for you until the spirits overwhelm the crew."

"Dammit, Wyrm, what would you have me do?" The captain rounded on her, tears leaking from both eyes, unheeded. "I have to accept that I can only save some of them, not all of them. Am I callous? You bet I am. I need to keep as many alive as I can, for as long as I can. I need to keep my son alive, and if they kill us he's next. So yeah, those poor kids will keep dying, so that their friends and shipmates don't have to."

Visala suffered a rare moment of regret. Perhaps she'd spoken hastily. Did she really have a better option to offer? What might she have done had she the key? She didn't know, but it meant judging this woman's actions might be unfair.

"Excuse me," came a polite, cultured voice from behind the pair of them. A voice she'd never thought to hear again. "My name is Inura. You might be expecting me. I believe your son Jerek mentioned I was coming."

"No, I definitely would have remembered that." The captain might have been gaping at the newly appeared god, but Visala didn't know.

She couldn't look away from her grandfather. He lived. Somehow he lived. And he'd found her. If it indeed was him. She must be wary.

"Do you have some way to prove your identity?" Visala demanded. She slid her feet apart and prepared for combat, should it come to that.

"Other than translocating onto your bridge?" Inura raised an eyebrow in a manner she'd never forget. "By the Wyrmmother...is that you, little Visala?" His face lit up in a smile. "I suppose I can't call you little any longer. You're larger than I am."

"Larger? What do you mean?" She couldn't process what she was hearing. Couldn't fathom the idea of him being alive.

"I am...less than I was. I sacrificed my body in the Battle of the Fist to convince my enemies I am dead."

"And now you've lost that advantage by coming out of hiding." Visala horrified herself with the scorn in that tone. "At least you are here. Do you have the strength to reinforce the wards, or to reinforce the core?"

"You made this ship, right?" The captain pressed in on Inura. "If you can't empower the wards, do you know of any tactics or defenses we can employ? What does my son mean when he says you are a god?"

Inura eyed the door as if seeking escape. Fury roared through Visala as she took in his cowardly demeanor. What had happened to her once mighty grandfather? This was a shadow...less than a shadow.

"I can empower the wards for a time, long enough to block a shot." He looked up suddenly. "I might be able to do it twice, but to be candid, if your son fails to return with the core I cannot turn the tide in a battle with that perverted monstrosity. We need a way to hit back, and I cannot do that. I can only prolong the inevitable."

Visala contained her anger. Whatever this thing was, whatever it claimed, it wasn't her grandfather. Still, she'd welcome whatever help this simpering demigod could provide.

Almost she wished he had died at the Fist, his legacy and memory untarnished.

21

The lift doors opened, and we entered a mezzanine nearly identical to every other I'd seen thus far, except that this one was without power. Nothing moved. No sound broke the silence, save the O_2 scrubbers, which wouldn't keep the atmosphere breathable for very long without the cores to power the planet.

"Seket, this is Jerek." I trotted out ahead of the others, and used my vision to scout. A few shamblers approached, but we'd emerged into an area largely devoid of unliving. "We're on the surface and ready for pickup. Are you in a position to come get us?"

"Affirmative," Seket's golden voice rang back. "I am on my way. All drones have been dealt with, and I haven't seen any threats since the planet went dark. You didn't mention that would happen if you stole the core."

"We didn't know." I directed everyone over to a docking tube, the one I suspected would be most convenient for Seket. "There's a lot to catch you up on, but your

Maker was involved. He saved our lives when the casing on the core blew."

"Then you are blessed. I will be there swiftly, Captain. Seket out."

The comm went silent and left the squad standing around waiting. Normally that's not an issue. When you are at the ragged edge of exhaustion, though, it's a nightmare. All I wanted to do was rest my head against the wall and sleep, but I knew if I did it I'd be down for at least six hours.

So I paced. Back and forth, back and forth.

Briff and Rava chatted in low tones. Anger rolled off her, and I didn't blame her for seething. I hadn't realized you could skip *life* magic in exchange for appearance.

I mean, not that I wouldn't want to be more attractive. It would be awesome to suddenly be hotter. But if you have to pick between Seket's jawline and magically healing your friends in dangerous situations, it's not a hard choice.

"Jerek!" A friendly, cultured, and all too familiar voice echoed across the mezzanine. "Hello! Do you have a moment to chat before you leave?"

I turned to see our necromancer friend on his bone harness, with dragon in tow. He scuttled backwards a few paces when Briff took a threatening step in his direction.

The soulshackled Wyrm moved to intercept Briff, and its inferno eyes narrowed.

"Now, now." The necromancer waved, and the Wyrm retreated. "I just wanted to congratulate you on your victory. You somehow survived, and managed to disable this moon. Well done. It's really quite impressive for a—and I do not mean this insultingly—child."

"Is there a reason I shouldn't tattle to Inura?" I rested my hand on my pistol, but I'm fairly certain he knew I was just posturing.

"Translocation can only be performed once every few hours or so. Your god cannot help you." He offered a friendly smile completely at odds with his horrific body. "After you survive this ordeal and return to your ship you will want answers. I see the unquenchable thirst for knowledge in you. Who are these unliving? Why did they arise now? If you want answers...come to Sanctuary. Seek the unseen fleets, and you'll find them. Come, and I will teach you. Prepare you."

I almost asked him what he got out of all this, but realized he'd just spew some cryptic politician non-answer. I couldn't handle it right now.

"Hey, that sounds great. I'll see you on Sanctuary. I'll bring the beer. Totally. Just hang out 'til I get there." And then I turned from him. Petty, maybe. Even a little stupid. But I figured if this guy wanted to attack us he would have already done so.

"I get the sense that you question my motives." The necromancer scuttled a bit closer. "A sign of my intentions, then. My true name is Utred. I haven't ever trusted that to a living soul. You have an ally in me, child. And now...I will have the last word. If I could offer one final piece of advice. Be far from the *Word of Xal* when Necrotis comes for it. Inura will not stop her. He could not even stop me."

I heard a hum behind me, and turned to see a slash in

reality that led into the spirit realm. Utred scuttled through, and it closed behind the strange necromancer.

"Do you take him at his word?" Kurz wondered. Nothing in his tone indicated how he felt one way or the other.

"Of course not," Vee answered for me. "He's smarter than that."

"I don't trust him, but I do wonder why someone powerful enough to recognize and stand up to Inura wants to be buddies. It seems a little strange he's taken an interest to me, or that he's trying to drive up tourism to whatever death trap he lives in."

"I don't trust him," Vee repeated.

"You don't trust the evil necromancer?" Rava rolled her eyes. "It's odd that you don't trust this guy, but are cool with soulcatchers. I don't understand the distinction."

"I'm not going to try to explain." Vee shook her head. "I doubt you're really interested in the answer anyway."

"The distinction," Kurz interrupted in a friendly tone, "is that soulcatchers only take the souls of the fallen. We do not murder others to take or use their souls, and we do not bind souls into unliving bodies."

I knew I wasn't involved in that part of the conversation, but hearing that eased the moral discomfort in my chest. I should probably break up the argument, but exhaustion kept my jaw firmly shut.

The rush of engines vibrated through the wall as the *Remora* descended into view and docked against the tube. I leaned against the wall next to the panel as I waited for it to connect, and wished that I could collapse once we got inside.

It's never that easy. We still needed to get the core past the necromancers, and aboard the *Word*. I didn't want to risk communicating that we were carrying the core, so we could make the approach stealthily.

"Seket, have you been watching the orbital battle? Anything to report?"

"The *Wrath* fired on the *Word* about two minutes ago." Seket's tone thickened with worry. "It appears their wards stopped some or all of the shot, but it was a near thing. I believe the next shot may be fatal to the crew."

"I'll meet you on the bridge, and we'll see if we can stop that. Jerek out." The airlock doors opened, and I sprinted inside. I had to stop this. Had to help them before my mother, and the rest of my friends, were murdered as fuel for Necrotis.

22

By the time we made it onto the *Remora*'s bridge, Seket had already disengaged from the dock and lifted back into the air. The scry-screen showed the compact spaceport below us, and the clusters of wights roaming it in search of victims.

Most of the horde appeared to have moved on, probably heading deeper into the enclave-cities where the wealthy lived, as they were the most likely survivors. And thanks to us they were without power.

I reminded myself that we'd only hastened the inevitable, but it still weighed more than I would have liked.

The *Remora* accelerated, and we climbed away from the doomed moon, unencumbered by atmospheric friction, though we still contended with gravity.

Seket stumbled, but caught himself against the matrix's stabilizing ring. "I'm sorry, Captain, but I am not sure if I can continue. My magic is gone. I can no longer power the wards. You may want another pilot for what comes next."

I closed my eyes and willed the mask to slither from my face. The HUD didn't work anyway, and I needed to breathe air that hadn't been anywhere near that moon.

"Our options," I explained aloud as I worked through the problem, "are Briff, Rava, Miri, or myself."

"I'm not a pilot." Miri shook her head. "I'm a bad choice."

"If I'd gotten *life* magic I'd volunteer." Rava tugged on her jacket, which she'd put on over her armor. "Guess I'll just stand here and look pretty. *Fire* isn't going to cut it on those engines. We need *void*. Or *life*."

"Listen to you rambling on about magic." I gave her a proud smile. "That leaves Briff or myself. I'll take this one, bud. I've got some flying experience. It's not much, but it might make a difference."

"It's okay, Jer. It's a good call." Briff clapped me on the shoulder, and knocked me forward a half step. "You're faster than I am too. I know you'll get us back to the *Word*."

Seket tumbled out of the matrix gracefully, and Rava darted forward to catch him. Miri joined her, and the pair carried the paladin over to one of the hovercouches lining the side of the bridge.

I allowed a single pensive breath, then ducked into the rings. My fingers flew over the *life* sigils on all three rings, and just like that the ship and I were one once more. The connection differed, though.

Void allowed precise, minute movements. *Life* produced

huge amounts of thrust, but relied on the pilot's skill to direct them. It was much more like a flight simulator, and less thinking about where you wanted to go and being there.

That was fine. I liked flight simulators.

The difference between my skill and Seket's was obvious, but at least I could fly the *Remora* competently. And hey, if we lived, then this counted as practice.

In the distance a trio of wedge-shaped fighters approached, each tiny even beside the *Remora*, one of the smallest starships. That size didn't reflect their lethality. It just made them more difficult targets.

"Erect your wards," Seket called weakly from the hovercouch.

"Right." I tapped *life* all three times, and winced as the vessel drew magical star stuff from my chest. Golden magic rolled out of me, and into the floor of the matrix.

I willed the wards to activate, and my magic surged through them in a latticework of tiny sigils. Not three seconds later the fighters screamed into range, and unleashed a trio of void bolts.

At my command the *Remora* abruptly changed course, and dodged two of the three bolts. The third slammed into our wards. The magic weakened, but held as we shot past all three fighters.

They were already coming around, but it would take them a minute to reach us again. That gave me time to think, and maybe come up with a plan. We were larger, but slower and less maneuverable. That kind of fight only ended one way.

"Vee," I called, my senses still subsumed under the ship's perceptions. "Can you look for a mana potion?

Anything in the schematics or existing supplies that can give me a bit of pool?"

"On it." Vee raced off the bridge and up the corridor to the mess.

I didn't hold out much hope that she'd find anything, but if she did it could add *void* back into the mix for me.

The *Remora* tore through the black at incredible speeds, but I already knew I couldn't reach the *Word* before the enemy fighters would get another try for us. This time, though, they could maneuver into our back-field and stay there as they peppered us with spells.

I could flip the ship and fly in their direction, but then I'd be flying away from our destination, and that afforded them more chances to kill us, or to bring more fighters.

The *Remora* rumbled as a volley of spells streaked out from the fighters, but miraculously my wards held. I tapped the *life* sigils once more and reinforced them, but another volley quickly depleted them. I was quickly running out of *life* magic.

"Jer!" Vee came skidding back onto the bridge with a bright blue vial in her hands. "I've got a mana potion. No beer involved, but it will replenish raw magic."

"Oh, you are amazing." I extended a hand to the edge of the rings and she passed it through. I removed the stopper with my thumb, and upended the contents, which tasted of blueberries.

Potent rolling magic swirled in my gut, then suffused my body. A bit of *fire*, a bit of *void*, a bit of *dream* and a bit of *life* all rose within me, ready to heed my call.

Right now all I needed was the *void*.

As the necrotech fighters began their next assault I

tapped the *void* sigils on all three rings, then willed the spelldrive to teleport. We vanished a moment before the spells would have connected, and re-appeared in the backfield behind the fighters.

I switched to *life*, and cored the first fighter with a life bolt. The fragile thing exploded, but the other two fighters peeled off before I could aim. That was fine by me. I poured on the speed, and pushed hard for the *Word of Xal*.

The fighters came back around, but they were distant, and we'd very nearly reached the *Word*'s protective guns. They kept after us anyway, and fired again when they reached range.

I blinked again, this time closer to the *Word*. Their spells sailed harmlessly through the space we'd occupied, while we flew into the *Word*'s protective shadow.

The last two fighters peeled off, and winged back toward the *Maker's Wrath*.

I'd just flown my combat mission, and *we'd lived*.

My elation died as we sailed into the *Word*'s cargo hold, and I saw an utterly massive bone thief surging toward a trio of young mages in the far corner, probably first year students.

23

I reached for the magic now coiling within me as I tapped *life* and *fire* on the spell matrix's gold and silver sigils, and fed much of my newly restored power into the highest magnitude spell I could cast.

An unforgiving beam of scarlet-gold brilliance streaked into the bone thief, and eradicated thousands of bugs, and several of the wicked skulls.

I switched to pure *fire* to finish off the stragglers, and finally relaxed a hair when the kids appeared to be safe. All three held weapons, and had been holding their own, as much as anyone could.

It took the last of my focus and concentration to land the ship, and an awful pounding took residence behind my temples as the first migraine I'd suffered in some time began to build.

At least it would keep me awake long enough to do what we had to.

"Let's move, people," I slurred as the ship lumbered to

a halt. The bone thief hadn't reformed, so I disconnected from the ship.

Everyone had already filed off the bridge, so I ducked through the rings and followed them toward the cargo bay.

I raised a trembling hand and sketched a *fire* sigil, then a *dream*, then another *fire*. They fused into a missive spell, and by the time I entered the cargo bay a blessedly beautiful face had appeared on the scry-screen along one wall.

"Mom," I croaked as I leaned into the stabilizing ring. "Minister is sleeping safely. She's had a sedative and will be out for hours. We recovered some magic, but not nearly as much as we were hoping. A mostly depleted reactor."

There was so much more I could say, but I wanted to give her time to respond, and ask whatever she deemed important. I'd deferred to command to her, after all, and that wasn't in name only. My mother was the captain of this ship, and I'd treat her as that rank warranted. Also words were hard right now.

"How do you plan to introduce it into the system?" Stress applied enormous pressure to her tone, though it didn't make it as far as her face. Her Heka Aten's mask was down for the moment.

"Just like I did the ship," I offered. "We teleport it directly into the drive. The ship eats it, and then we've got juice for the shields, and maybe enough to hit them back."

"I don't know, Jerek." Vee scratched anxiously at her cheek, and avoided eye contact. "That much magic all at once could blow a drive, even on a ship like this. Magic transmutes, sure, but you're only supposed to use sympathetic magic. For *void* that's either *earth* or *fire*. You can get away with *dream* or *spirit*, and maybe even *water* and *air*, but *life*? Transmuting an opposite will be a violent war for dominance, and it will yield the least amount of magic possible."

"All true." I rubbed my temples, and ran the numbers. I considered the data gathered when I'd fed the Inuran cruiser to it. If my math was correct, then the drive was about twelve times larger than the previous amount of magic we'd introduced. That wouldn't go very far, but it also seemed unlikely to endanger the ship. "I don't like it. It's risky. But less risky than taking a hit from the *Wrath* without our wards in place. We saw what the wights did on the surface, and there were...worse things."

Mom glanced off screen, and this time the worry did show on her face. Her mouth worked, and she brushed a stray lock of hair from her face. "The *Wrath* is charging their cannon. They'll be able to fire in the next few minutes. We're out of time."

"What do you want me to do?" I moved to stand next to the crate. We both knew she'd been trapped into a single logical answer.

"Do it." She killed the missive, presumably to tend to the damage I was about to cause.

"Rava, Miri." I turned to the pair, who'd been lounging near the ramp. "Get out there and reassure those kids. Bring them inside, and give them access to one of the unused rooms."

Rava nodded. Miri stabbed the button to activate the

ramp, then followed my sister into the *Word*'s cargo hold. The stench wafted in immediately, charred deadbug. It did awesome things to my head, let me tell you. Smell sensitivity is something I wouldn't wish on my worst enemy.

The trouble was my HUD had been shattered, and while I knew the system could repair it I suspected it would be many hours before that occurred. My suit needed rest as badly as I did, but the job wasn't done. Not yet.

"Guardian?" I called, and waited for him to manifest.

"Yes, Officer Jerek?" Kemet appeared with a magnificent pair of staff sparkles.

"Can we port directly to the bridge? And have we identified infected areas of the ship? Are those walled off with salt lines?" I forced myself to stem the tide of questions long enough for him to answer.

"We have partially identified areas where spirits roam." Kemet adopted a very Briff-like expression of chagrin. "Sensors are down over much of the ship. We've lost control of roughly 64% of the vessel. Areas of control center around the bridge and the cargo hold where Highspire resides. The corridor between them is well patrolled, but dangerous. If you teleport it will mitigate that danger, and save time, but is a significant drain on resources."

"Let's see what kind of resources we're talking about." I rubbed my gauntlets together, and forced the words. "Teleport the Inuran core into the ship's reactor."

"Ah, of course, Officer." A single staff sparkle this time.

The air warped and spun around the core, and then it was gone. The results were nearly immediate. The entire ship began to shake, and about four seconds later sparks flew from every light, and every console as systems burnt out all over the ship.

Dammit. My bad.

I willed the *Remora* to tap into the *Word*'s sensors, and had it feed the scrying spell directly to our screen. The *Wrath*'s spellcannon hummed with a hellish glow, one I well recognized from the last shot.

A stream of unnatural death flowed toward the *Word*, but the wards flared to brilliant life, and the blow shunted aside. On and on the flow of souls went, but the wards never slackened, or dimmed.

"All right!" I fist pumped. No one can tell me that isn't cool. I don't care what anyone says. "Time for some payback."

I waited for my mother to order the cannon to cast the mother of all disintegrates, and to finally even the score. Instead we simply sat there, not responding.

Should I missive her again? No she had plenty of things to deal with. Maybe the core had done more damage than I'd calculated? Maybe it had disabled critical systems?

Uh oh.

A missive tugged at my attention, and I willed it to display on the scry-screen. My mother's harried face appeared once more. She rubbed her temples in exactly the same way I had a few minutes before.

"Jer, we've got a problem." She looked up, eyes bloodshot, and crowfeet exaggerated. "The cannon is damaged.

We can see the relay that's causing the issue, but if those runes aren't repaired...there's no way we're going to be able to hit them back. Eventually they'll get through our shields, and all the while they're consolidating that moon, and picking off our crew."

"We're not going to let that happen. Can you transmit the location of the damage?" I forced a grim smile, for Mom's benefit. We had the answer to this problem. "Vee is an incredibly gifted artificer and engineer. We'll get that cannon back online. Just keep them off our backs."

Vee met my gaze. "I'm ready."

I willed the *Word* to teleport me and Vee from the *Remora*'s cargo hold to the conduit my mom had indicated on the schematics. I considered bringing more people, but each one exponentially increased the cost of the spell, and it wasn't like I'd dumped a ton of magic into the ship. We needed to conserve what my team had provided.

Vee and I appeared in a tube with black walls, broken by millions of tiny runes that covered every available space. The level of detail defied mortal description.

Large swathes of runes had gone dark, especially in the area we'd arrived in. A good twenty-meter gap separated the chains of sigils, which I took for a bad thing. "I assume we need to connect the sigils?"

"Exactly." Vee knelt and began sketching a sigil, which drew a tiny amount of *life* out of her. "We need to connect, then strengthen, a conduit of runes to bridge the damaged area."

"Can I use *dream* to draw these?" I moved to the opposite area, and knelt while awaiting a reply.

"I think so." Vee bit her lip. "It isn't ideal, but if you don't have *life* or *air*, that will do. They'll probably cook away the first time we fire."

I reached for *dream* and began drawing. The wrong tool for the job, just like I felt most of the time. But the wrong tool could still get the job done.

Each sigil took concentration and precision, which are pretty much the opposite of exhaustion. My hands trembled violently, and more than once I had to wipe a rune away and redraw the sigil.

I paused to start the next, but hesitated when I heard something in the distance. A low moaning, like soft wind through the stacks. Only...there was no wind inside of a starship.

"Contact," I hissed, then rose to my feet and drew my pistol. "Keep fixing the runes. I'll hold them off."

It was all bravado, I assure you. I had no idea what was coming, and had already seen some things I couldn't deal with on my own. My team was elsewhere now, my one companion unable to even defend herself.

I needed to hold the line, but I was a scholar. Wasn't I?

It seemed a strange moment for a life-defining moment, but there it was, seconds away from combat with an unknown foe. My identity had always been scholar. Relic hunter. Archeologist. Gamer. Slacker.

But I'd pulled off some crazy shit. I'd fought and killed mercs, wights, and worse. Maybe I could deal with whatever was coming, and maybe not, but I wouldn't be facing it as a scholar. I'd be facing it with Dez in my hand, and a spell in the barrel.

Or a salt round.

Relief washed away my brittle combat edge as a trio of wights surged up the barrel of the spellcannon. It was only wights. Only. Ha. They began their screeching wail the moment they saw me, and rushed in my direction.

I already had a bead on them, and squeezed the trigger twice. Two wights went up in puffs.

The third surged forward, and my next shot went wide as it flung spectral arms around me. I don't have words for the agony that bubbled up in my gut, and climbed toward my lungs, as the frigid embrace numbed me.

In the dimmest, oldest part of the animal brain something screamed that I must not let this happen. The consequences meant more than death. I'd be damned. Doomed to inflict the same fate on all living things until someone or something put me to rest.

I corrected my aim and squeezed Dez's trigger once more. A salt round exploded millimeters from my face, and coated my skin and hair with a salty, sickly residue that instantly triggered a gag reflex. I missed my helmet so much.

"Everything okay?" Vee called absently, her back to the combat. There wasn't a doubt in her mind that I'd deal with whatever came.

"Magical," I gasped, hand clutching my chest. I knew she was out of *life*, but I still had a little left. Could I really heal myself? That seemed crazy. I laid a hand on my breastplate, and willed the *life* to stir within me. It did, and the same brilliance Vee used rippled through the armor and took away some of the pain the wights had brought.

I rose and hobbled back over, elated that it was over.

A keening wail began up the barrel in the direction the wights had come from. The kind of overlapping wail that issued from dozens of throats.

"No pressure, but we need this done now." I knelt and began sketching the next sigil. Less than a meter separated my work from Vee's, but it felt like kilometers.

"Faster if you help." Vee didn't look at me, instead continuing to artfully sketch sigils as she connected the runes.

I did my best to keep up, but she drew three to my one. The line crept closer, and closer.

And in that moment I realized I'd been a moron. I'd been letting the stress and tension cloud my judgement.

I had salt rounds. We were enclosed in a magical barrel that wights couldn't pass through. If I put down a salt line...we would be safe.

I shoved Dez in my holster, and reached for a magazine of salt rounds. I popped three into my hand, and then used the suit's gauntlet to crush the relatively weak casing.

Wights flowed up the barrel towards us, dozens upon dozens, and behind them skittered another ivory-skinned necromancer. How had they known we were here? What possible other reason could they have had for being here?

I dropped to one knee, and began dribbling grains of salt as I created the first line. I'd barely finished when the wights reached it, and came up short close enough to touch me if not for the barrier.

Ignoring them and dropping another line of salt might have been the toughest fear I'd faced to that point. Everything in me screamed to cut and run, but logic won out. Run where? Running meant death.

I dropped another salt line, then mechanically opened more rounds, and drew another. I kept going until I reached ten, and tried to ignore the fact that the necromancer hadn't reacted.

Surely she had spells that would get past a few salt lines, but she merely lurked behind her minions and watched.

So I drew Dez and started executing wights, one after another. "How's it coming back there?" Somehow I kept the panic from my voice.

"Well," Vee called back, her tone self-critical. "It isn't my best work but it's connected. I'd like to spend some time strengthening it. Can you hold them a bit longer?"

"Maybe." My voice easily rose a half octave as I locked eyes with the necromancer. "Can you make it quick?"

Vee hummed softly to herself as I emptied the magazine, and then inserted another. More wights moved to replace the ones I'd killed, though none had made it past the first salt line.

"What are you doing?" The necromancer called in a melodious voice, her voice making the ancient draconic into lilting poetry. "Repairing the cannon? You must know that I can merely damage another section. And you can't escape. Yet you struggle on. Is it ignorance? Are you unaware of the forces arrayed against you? Or hubris? You truly believe you can win."

"I've won every fight so far," I taunted, though my inner monologue instantly corrected me with the dozen or so fights I had quite clearly lost in my brief career. "If you have the power to stop us why are we alive? You necromancers are a chatty bunch. Do you have a name, by the way?"

"My name?" she asked mildly. "Or the name of our people?"

"Both, if you don't mind." I stopped offing wights for a moment, and gave a friendly wave of my pistol. "I'm Jerek. You're running out of wights."

That wasn't really true. She had dozens remaining and I'd killed like...eight. If this ever becomes a holo, though, then I killed like forty. Forty-eight.

"I'll manage." She scuttled a bit closer, and I realized her jawline and the cast of her eyes reminded me a lot of Miri. If I needed confirmation these people were Inuran, there it was. "Are you willing to share your plan? It might buy you time. I am intensely curious. Why not flee? Why not both attack? You proceed as if...as if minerals sprinkled in my path will ward off my horde. I simply don't understand."

"Sure, I'll share." Oh, shit. How did I keep this lady talking? What was my grand plan? I went full stream of consciousness. "You have lovely hair. Anyway, the plan comes down to stakes. We're probably dead. Salt won't stop you, but it does stop your energetic kids. If I'm going to die then I choose to operate as if the possibility of victory still remains. There's a parable on my world of some poor magic-less sap falling off a cliff. He grabs at the few blades of grass as he goes over, even though he knows they won't save him. He's trying to live."

"Or she." The necromancer raised an eyebrow.

"Sure," I allowed. "Or she."

"No, you were right." She folded her arms. "She wouldn't be stupid enough to tumble off the cliff in the first place."

"Okay, so he then. He tries to save himself, even though he knows it will fail." I raised my pistol and executed another wight. "I'm doing the same. I want my death to matter, and there's an ember in me that won't be extinguished. Hope. We could win somehow. Crazier things have happened."

"Okay." Vee rose to her feet and scrubbed her hands against her pants to clean the sweat. "They're connected. I think we can fire, if this was the only blockage."

"I didn't catch your name," I politely inquired, operating as if Vee hadn't spoken.

"Ner—"

"Yeah, I don't care." I triggered a missive to my mom, and waited an eternity as it connected. "Mom, fire the cannon. Now."

"You're still in the cannon," she protested.

"Just do it! Please!" There wasn't any time to explain.

Thankfully my mother trusted me, and she proved it then. The runes all along the walls began to glow, and my new friend's eyes widened. Then she scuttled back as quickly as she could.

Me? I cheated. I willed the *Word* to teleport Vee and I to the bridge.

I materialized onto the *Word*'s bridge and took a moment to wipe the wight residue from my face. My eyes landed first on Inura, who'd planted himself a few paces from the spell matrix, hands clasped behind his back and wings resting regally over his shoulders.

There was no sign of the headmistress, though she'd been here the last time I'd missived. My mother stood in the vessel's spell matrix, and had just tapped the final *void* sigil.

She was about to use this vessel as the weapon of war for which it had been intended, and as I glanced at the scry-screen I glimpsed the target of her retribution. The *Maker's Wrath* hovered before us. The rival Great Ship's cannon glowed with the same hellish beam I'd seen vented on the moon.

The *Word* fired first.

A bolt of negative light streaked into the enemy vessel directly over what should be aft engines. An interlocking sea of wards sprang into visibility over the hull, their complexity humbling to a mage of my limited skill.

But not to a disintegrate launched by the vessel forged by multiple gods of artificing. The spell tore through the wards, and then through the *Wrath*'s hull. Bone and metal and worse things exploded into the black as one of three engines powered by the soul drive went dark.

The spell overpowered the enemy vessel's magical grid, if it had such a thing, because the energy that had been building in the enemy cannon withered and died entirely.

"Yes!" My mother did a fist pump inside the matrix. "We took the best they had, and came back swinging."

I'd never seen the bloodlust side of her before. She'd put all that aside long before I'd been old enough to understand what Arena was.

"Nice work, Captain." I saluted her, then raised an arm to indicate Vee. "This is my ship's engineer, friend, and...this is Vee."

My mother sized her up, a Wyrm about to dive on prey. She'd grilled all four of the dates I'd brought home like it was her big day in court and they were hostile witnesses. She kept her tongue though, which impressed me. "It's a pleasure, Vee. Thank you for keeping my son alive."

"Keeping *him* alive?" She jerked a thumb in my direction, and offered my mom an amused smile. "He keeps us alive. It's a pleasure to meet you, ah, what should I call you?"

"Captain," my mother interjected frostily. Not the

answer I'd expected. She turned back to the scry-screen. "We'll catch up after the battle. We need to finish them."

The Guardian appeared with a grave staff sparkle. "Pardon, Captain, but the cannon will not fire again without further repairs. Discharging a spell has eradicated many previously damaged runes. I estimate fourteen hours to full repair. Perhaps eight hours to limited functionality, if repairs begin immediately."

My mother's mouth firmed into a determined line. "We have no idea how soon they'll be able to fire on us, but I'm guessing they'll fix their problem before we fix ours. Visala returned to Highspire. Please tell the headmistress that her students will need to repair the cannon."

I wondered if my necromancer friend—Ner—had survived. Unless she had teleported, or escaped into the spirit realm, that beam had seemed pretty lethal. If I'd failed to kill her she might hold a grudge. Eh, I was pretty sure that would never come back to haunt me.

My eye twitched as the migraine ratcheted up another octave. At first I thought it was my brain's last feeble protest about the lack of sleep, but the insistent buzzing changed my mind. My vision had activated, and seemed mighty perturbed about something.

I glanced to my right, over Vee's shoulder, and saw a vertical tear slowly open in reality. It lay in the bridge's far corner, in the dimmest part of the room, but it still should have caught my mom's attention. And Vee's. And Inura's. And the guards'.

Wait, there weren't any guards. My mother was on the bridge...effectively alone since Inura the distracted still peered at the scry-screen, oblivious to his surroundings.

A tall soldier in bleached armor and a menacing skull mask strode through the tear. He carried a unique black rifle with a long barrel, and a canister strapped to that side. My vision showed me exactly what that canister contained, and my stomach joined the protest as I realized his rifle ate souls as ammunition.

He raised his rifle. The motion part of his stance, part of his gait...everything about how this solider moved screamed professional master. I'd run across people like this in Arena every now and then. Just when you started to feel like you were somebody this guy would show up and take apart your whole team.

Only this wasn't a game. And my team was also my family.

I wrapped both hands around Dez's grip and thumbed the selector back to spells. I still had *dream*, and if this guy was dead it would act like a void bolt. If not, and it put him to sleep, well, that worked too.

I assumed I'd be his first target as I was the only one reacting, but when his rifle snapped to his shoulder, and became an extension of his body, the barrel wasn't aimed at me. It lay centered over my mother's face, behind me and to the right.

This was an assassin, not a strike team. A disposable weapon with one purpose. Kill the target. Kill the captain of the *Word of Xal*. In giving up the power, I'd also painted a target on the person who'd brought me into this world.

"No!" Dez snapped up a hair's breadth after my opponent's rifle. It wasn't going to be enough.

I hurled myself into the path of the spell, and caught it with my shoulder before it reached the matrix. Numb soul-shackling agony, twin to what I'd experienced when the wight grabbed me, lanced through my shoulder and into my chest.

My entire body went rigid as the spell overcame me, and I collapsed to the deck, paralyzed.

Vee never moved or reacted. Neither did my mother. In the distance I could hear her rattling orders to the ship as she maneuvered the ship to put the trade moon between us and the *Wrath*.

That revealed to our enemies that our spellcannon couldn't fire, and I wanted to yell that, but my muscles refused to obey.

The assassin's soulrifle came up again, and not even Inura seemed aware of his presence. The rifle kicked, and I scrunched my eyes shut. Not to block it out, but to concentrate.

My body refused to obey, because the *spirit* magic had me in its grip. I still possessed *dream* magic, which, as we've established, was the opposite. In theory, *dream* could directly counter *spirit*, and would be used by a talented mage were they counter spelling.

Spellarmor is a focus for spells. Normally I have to painstakingly draw sigils in the air. I need to will the magic into existence. Spellweapons and spellarmor remove the need for spellcasting, which is why they exist.

I fed *dream* into the armor, and the pressure immediately lessened on my chest. My arm twitched.

Too late. A pallid grey spell slammed into my mother's unprotected head, and she toppled into the rings with a cry. Then she tumbled to the floor, limbs limp beside her. Not dead, I prayed, but paralyzed as I was.

I fed the suit more *dream*.

Inura spun, and a blazing sword of light appeared in one hand as he advanced on the reaper. "Clever, using the spirit realm. Your tear must have been incredibly subtle, or there's a greater power at work here. Necrotis veiled your approach, didn't she?"

The reaper didn't answer. He tossed his rifle to the ground, and slid his hand through a tear into the spirit world. It emerged clutching a blade that hurt my eyes to look at, the dark metal's spiteful gleam a stain on our reality.

I rose shakily to my feet as Inura closed with the assassin, and they began to duel. I don't know what I expected. Some part of me expected Inura to be a master swordsman, and he was skilled, but not noticeably better than the reaper.

Quite the opposite. The reaper focused more on chopping with powerful blows, which forced Inura to dance back and give ground, without offering much in return.

I raised Dez and gave her the last of my *dream*. "If you've got a way to juice spells now is the time."

We. Save!

Purple-black energy crackled in the barrel, then Dez hurled my dream bolt into the back of the assassin's head. I didn't recognize the *void* or *fire* infusing the spell, but the effect was pretty easy to measure.

The spell knocked the reaper forward a step, and then

melted the back of his skull. I won't describe the rest, because who needs that visual?

The assassin clattered to the deck, Inura's panting form standing victoriously over him as if he'd delivered the killing blow.

"I hope this was her most useful servant." Inura spat on the corpse. "This was a grasping attempt to regain control of the situation, and it failed. Mark my words... she will run now. We have driven her from the field."

I didn't really even know who he was delivering his speech to. Vee politely listened, her face a mask of shock as she stared at the pooling blood. I didn't. I rushed to my mother.

Two fingers to her throat confirmed that she still breathed, and I pulled her from the matrix. I couldn't heal her right now, but hopefully it had been the same paralysis spell that had affected me.

"*Dream* counters it," I explained to her as I pulled up against the stabilizing ring. "We can channel it through the armor."

My mother's eyes fluttered, and her face split into a weak grin. "Much better."

I rose to my feet and eyed the scry-screen. The *Maker's Wrath* hadn't fired, but neither had they retreated. I still had no idea what they were going to do, and if they attacked it would probably have to be me on the matrix.

This could still end messily.

I'd never get to go to bed.

INTERLUDE VI

Necrotis strode past her children and sat gracefully on the hovercouch. The others went unused, as both Utred and his sister Neria preferred their multi-limbed harnesses. She didn't doubt the necrotech's usefulness, but they did not provide enough advantage to mar her body, as her children had.

That troubling change spoke to the difference in her people. This was the place she'd led them. Beauty wasn't valued as much as power. Strength. Their bodies were vessels to be modified and discarded as needed. A very un-Inuran way to be, and yet one that had propelled people to great position upon her vessel.

"Will you flee?" Neria demanded. Always a demand. "If you run, the moon will have ample time to fester, but they could bring in a Confederate god to oversee extraction of the remaining Great Ships. We could lose everything else in this system."

"So you advocate staying." Necrotis gave a noncommittal nod. Acknowledgement, not agreement. "And you

Utred? What of your sister's counsel? Flee? Or destroy the vessel housing my father's wretched shadow, and the last who'd oppose us in this system?"

"You said we were impregnable." There was no rancor or accusation, just a matter-of-fact recitation. "We clearly are not. That they have not fired again suggests that either they lack the magic, or their ship is damaged. Given that the spellcannon has not been fired in ten millennia I'm guessing the latter."

"I was inside that weapon not twenty minutes ago." Neria folded her arms and scuttled forward on her harness, the spikes digging into the marble as they fought for purchase. Necrotis schooled her features to stillness, and ignored the damage. It could be repaired. "Your new pet tended to the worst of the damage, enough for the weapon to function, but after that monstrosity fired there are likely dozens of runic breaks. It will take them time to repair. If we strike now, then we could overwhelm them. Their cannon is useless if we fully infest their vessel."

Necrotis turned back to her scry-screen and studied the *Word of Xal*. She considered her father's words, and his expression. That he would defend these children until his dying breath went without question. Her father had always been a fool.

It seemed clear that he lacked his former strength, but underestimating him would make her the bigger fool. He'd built the *Word*. There were no doubt many tricks he could perform, and some of them might be the end of everything she'd worked to achieve.

And, if she was being honest, the Outrider she'd used to be begged clemency. Inura wasn't her enemy here. The

Consortium was. They'd paid for their arrogance and their treachery, and would continue to pay until the last soul was used as fuel.

"What of the boy?" She turned back to her eldest children. "Both of you took his measure. Is Utred's plan feasible? Can this relic hunter do what you require?"

"He can." Utred rapped his staff on the ground twice, offering respect. "He overcame a seasoned reaper under a veil you yourself constructed. That suggests he has the ability. He made if off the moon, despite nearly everyone on it dying. That suggests tenacity, and a will to live. He also disabled the moon's propulsion system, and acquired a core in the process. That shows ingenuity. He can think on his feet. If we point him at our problem he will solve it, if it can be solved."

"All problems can be solved." Necrotis willed the hovercouch into the air, and spun it to face the scry-screen. She'd badly wanted to add the *Word* to her growing armada, but that seemed an impossibility today. The question was...how best to resolve matters.

There were a few valid options. She could contact Inura, and offer a truce. Inura wouldn't listen, but the captain might. She seemed a pragmatic woman.

She could simply leave without a word. That sent its own message, and it said we are enemies, but we will settle this another day. Or she could attack and overwhelm them.

The last option was undoubtedly the smartest, were one working only with percentages. The odds that Inura could resist a full assault were slim. Flee, maybe. But fight back? Win? Almost nil. She possessed all the scales, save the tiny bunch in one surrounded corner that her father still controlled.

Yet she'd seen Inura in his prime. He excelled at empowering others. Inura hadn't been great. He'd made his sisters great. Virkonna, and Marid, and Nefarius, and the Earthmother had all profited from his knowledge and unrivaled skill.

What if he performed the same magic on the people around him? What if he worked with the Confederacy? Problems, perhaps, but she was borrowing trouble from the future.

"Neria." She tilted the couch in her daughter's direction. "You will stay. I charge you will harnessing the trade moon. Organize your armies, and prepare for war. Convert all you can, as quickly as you can. Expect a possible response within the week."

"And me?" Utred wondered. Always wondered, never demanded. She didn't know which she hated more.

"Lure the boy off that ship." She zoomed toward the matrix, and the broad-shouldered man currently powering their drive. "Bring him to Sanctuary. I will go there now to prepare the way, and to finalize our accord with the unseen fleets. Our flag will change, but our power will increase. More importantly we will be merely one threat among many."

"You fear Inura." Utred's tone expressed his surprise. "Or perhaps the Confederacy. These "gods" haven't been that for more than a year. They have no idea how to prosecute a real war. They have no idea what we are capable of. I often advise caution, but mother...Neria is right. Delaying only gives them time."

"Perhaps," she allowed, and hated it. "I will present the matter to the unseen, and their council will vote. We will be on that council, and our voice will be heard."

"Bring me ships," Neria sulked. "I will prepare your armies." She slashed the air, and stepped through the tear into the spirit realm.

Utred folded his arms, and turned back to the scry-screen. "I will bait the boy out. He will come to Sanctuary. If we are successful your caution will prove well founded, and cost us nothing. If we are wrong, though, that caution may doom us."

"Perhaps." Necrotis finally smiled. "I play a patient game, but unlike my father I am an aggressive opponent. They must see us as part of a faceless mass, a threat that must be overcome as a whole. That will force the unseen fleets to leave Sanctuary, and only then will the Confederacy realize the scope of the threat."

"I see." Utred scuttled a bit closer, and when he smiled she saw the boy she'd given birth to all those millennia ago. "I knew you had a stratagem. Grandfather won't be easily overcome, but if the Confederacy attacks the unseen fleets, the ensuing war will provide all the distraction we'll need. Again, assuming the boy is successful."

"Then go make him successful. I will wait until you are away before making the tear."

Her son scuttled away, an eager smile touching his lips, more emotion than he'd expressed in decades. She dearly hoped he didn't grow too attached to his newest pet. But then he always did.

And he was always heartbroken when they died.

26

I didn't remember making it to bed. I didn't remember anything after killing the assassin, now that I think about it. It took effort to raise my head from the pillow, and I realized I'd been carried back to my quarters in the *Remora*.

The sheet slid off me as I sat up and noted I still wore my armor. I wondered if the HUD was repaired, but not badly enough to don my helmet. As far as I was concerned this was a day off.

My job had been get Minister Ramachan back to the *Word*. I'd done that, with some extra magic, and kept my new/old boss/mom alive.

Footsteps sounded outside my hatch, which wide open. Vee's head poked in a moment later. "Oh, you're awake. Good. Your mom wants you to report to some sort of breakfast meeting they've set up."

"Just me?" My shoulders slumped.

"Just you." Vee laughed and shook her head. "There's

no way you could talk me into going. I'm spending twelve glorious hours working on a schematic for a second bracelet. I'm going to use it for defense, like a spellshield, but much more versatile."

"That sounds a whole lot more fun and useful than politics, or worse...mingling." I rose with a stretch. "I'll come poke my head in when I get back. I'd love to see a prototype if you build one."

Vee gave one more infectious smile, then headed off in the direction of the forge.

"Guardian, do you know where I'm supposed to report to meet the captain?" I willed my helmet to slither over my face, and gave a relieved sigh when the HUD lit up. A white line still marred the screen, but the worst of the damage had been repaired.

"Of course, Captain. I was told you might ask. You're to report to the *Spear of Seket*. The vessel is berthed nearby, making a short range teleport the most efficient means of travel."

"Great." I glanced around my quarters, but couldn't think of anything to contribute to a breakfast without some details ahead of time. I closed my eyes and willed the *Word* to teleport me to the *Spear of Seket*.

A night's rest had refilled my reserves, so I powered the spell myself. It felt good to flex my magical muscles, which had grown considerably in recent months. I only knew a handful of people with more than three Catalyzations—well, prior to getting more than three myself.

I appeared in the minister's ready room, which had been converted into a temporary officer's mess. My mother, Minister Ramachan, and Visala were all chatting as they heaped fruit, eggs, and bacon onto their plates. It looked to be the real stuff, too, and not a soy substitute.

Only after I'd surveyed the room did I order my mask to slither off. I was getting paranoid.

"Jer!" My mom gave an enthusiastic wave. "Come join us before we're interrupted by the next crisis. We're celebrating. The enemy withdrew."

I gave a relieved smile and sagged wordlessly into the chair opposite my mother. A night's sleep had done wonders, but I couldn't shake the grogginess.

"Have we taken steps to purge the spirits from the *Word*?" I scooped eggs onto a plate, and savored a bite while I awaited an answer.

"It isn't feasible." My mother deflated, and I noted the bags under her eyes. I also noted the empty champagne glass next to her plate. This wasn't breakfast for her. This was a celebratory dinner before bed. She sighed, and shook her head. "The amount of magic it would take would cripple the drive. We'd be stranded here. I had Guardian run the numbers, and then asked Visala to—"

"I can speak for myself," the headmistress groused. She gnawed on a piece of bacon, and her eyes never left it. "Your mother is right. Much as I hate it we cannot be rid of the spirits just yet. They infest parts of the ship, but my students have been trained to use salt lines, and are shoring up our defenses around the areas of the ship we control. It will be good practice for the older students to root out undead. We will retake the ship, eventually."

My mother blinked at that, then nodded. "Your pragmatism—"

"Is monstrous," I interrupted. "This isn't a training exercise, and these are not soldiers. These are students who just survived the destruction of their world. If you're taking volunteers, great, but you shouldn't force kids that aren't ready to face what's lurking in those corridors. We don't even know if the spirits are the worst of it. We've hardly explored this ship, and there could be anything out there."

"That I can agree with." My mother nodded, and I settled back into my chair. She popped a piece of watermelon into her mouth, a luxury provided by the *Spear*'s forge. "Volunteers only. In the meantime I'd like to see if you can gather flame readers to study Necrotis's movements. I want as much information as possible to present to Lady Voria when we arrive at Shaya."

"Arrive at Shaya?" I set down my fork. "I feel like I missed a strategy meeting or three. How long was I asleep?"

"We haven't left yet." My mother dabbed at her cheek with a napkin. "Which brings me to your role. I need you to open a Fissure, plot a course to Shaya, and get us underway. We're the only two people I want in that matrix, which means twelve-hour shifts."

I picked my fork up again, just for something to occupy me. My mother had just promoted me to first officer, without even asking, and without really offering the position.

"I'll take you to Shaya." My grip tightened on the fork. All the terror, and anger, and fear that had built during my time on the moon surged through me. This time, though, I controlled it. "I agree that Confederate aid is our only real hope, and they need to know about Necrotis and the *Wrath*."

"But?" Visala raised an eyebrow. I couldn't see her as an old woman after having faced her as a Wyrm.

"But I gave up being captain of this vessel." I leaned back in my chair, and fixed my mother with a firm stare. Strangely, she no longer intimidated me. "I have no official rank on this ship. I *do* have a rank on my ship, the *Remora*. Captain. I have a responsibility to my crew. After we arrive at Shaya I need to chart a course that reflects their needs. I can't be at your beck and call simply because I'm your son."

My mother leaned back in her chair, mirroring my pose. Her face became an emotionless mask, though at least there wasn't any anger, or even confusion. Beyond that I couldn't read her.

"You're right." She picked up another hunk of watermelon, and popped it in her mouth. After a moment's thoughtful chewing she continued. "We've been in crisis mode for—"

"No, he isn't right. Don't be preposterous." Minister Ramachan smoothed the sleeves of her business jacket, and gone was the smiling spouse happy to be reunited after a life-and-death situation. I judged her less harshly, though, having borne the weight of life and death decisions involving others so recently. It sucked. "Jerek, respectfully, that armor is linked to the ship. If you plan to go your separate ways, then we'll need you to relinquish the armor. You're one of two officers, and our only fallback should something, Maker forbid, happen to your mother."

A brilliant glow built a few meters from the table, and resolved into Inura, as if the deity's entrance had been timed to interrupt as dramatic a moment as possible. His wings flared behind him, and I noted he'd found time to change into elegant white clothing that draped off his wiry form. Not a good look. My dad would have lectured him to get his ass to the gym.

"I've come to say goodbye." Inura offered an elegant bow. "I am going to Voria to ask her to rally the pantheon, so we are likely to be reunited soon. In the meantime I have an...well, I'll just come right out and ask. Do you have the key? I sent Ardaki with Admiral Kemet to keep him as far from the *Spellship* as possible. That need has passed. With Ardaki I can return home an equal, and can show Voria what the vessel was truly created for."

"And without it," Visala slyly interjected, "you are nothing but a beggar, grandfather. A powerless beggar asking the gods with the real magic to please deal with the new threat you accidentally unleashed on the sector."

Inura winced as if slapped, and his guilty eyes fell to the floor. "An accurate, if a bit harsh, assessment of my current circumstances. However, I possess much in the way of knowledge. This new pantheon needs an advisor. One that remembers the last epoch from the point of view of a god."

In that moment I pitied him. He'd lost everything. His worshippers. His world. His own body. Any prestige or respect he'd once had.

"Thank you for your help on the trade moon." My words drew a grateful smile from the fallen god. "Please tell Voria that we'll make best time through the Depths and be there as soon as we can with more evidence. Please also let her know that our vessel is infested with spirits and worse."

"I will." Inura offered me a deep bow, then vanished.

27

I boarded the bridge of the *Word of Xal* the conventional way, and the walk there did loads for my confidence. There hadn't been any guards on the bridge, but there were pairs of blue-suited cadets at every intersection leading up to it. Most were my age, or a few years younger.

That didn't detract from their lethality or professionalism in any way. These mages had survived the fall of Kemet, the attack of Bortel's legions, and now wights... and worse. My mind strayed to the trio we'd saved from the bone thief. I didn't even know their names, and they'd already headed back to Highspire Hold.

The pair of cadets outside the door saluted as the doors slid shut and walled them off from me. Who did they think I was? I had no idea what rumors were circulating, or even who I'd ask. It wasn't so long ago I'd been a part of the student body. Now I was alien. Separate. An adult.

Yeah, it was weird.

I moved to the matrix and gave a grin of anticipation. The universe looked a whole lot different after a night's sleep. I had *life* magic. I'd lived. My people had lived. We had a new crew member, one I found interesting.

The doors slid open again, and I glanced in mild surprise to see Vee enter. I ducked into the matrix as she approached, and carefully tapped each *void* sigil to link to the ship. I'd need *void* specifically to open a Fissure.

"Mind if I watch?" Her hair bobbed behind her as a tentative smile crept onto her face. "I've never been through a Fissure, much less seen the Umbral Depths. Seems like this is the safest opportunity. I mean, if you don't mind the company. We haven't really talked since we...got off."

She looked away at those last words. I didn't need to ask why. I hadn't even begun to unpack everything we'd witnessed. All that carnage. The screams in that subway tunnel....

"I'd love the company." I closed my eyes briefly as the vessel bonded me. For a time I'd thought it the other way around, but more and more it felt like I was the junior partner in the relationship. "I've never been in the Depths either, and they worry me. If I get the course off by even a fraction of a degree...our heading could put us off the main pathways and there's no way to recover. We'd be lost. Best case we could blind jump back to our reality and try to get our bearings, but we could come out anywhere."

"Or nowhere." Vee shuddered and looked up again. "I hear some ships don't emerge, and aren't ever heard from again."

"Being aboard a Great Ship helps." I patted the stabilizing ring. "If we tried this on the *Remora* I'd be a lot more terrified. I can't imagine anything wanting to tangle with a ship this large."

"Pardon, Officer Jerek." The Guardian appeared suddenly, staff in hand, though with no sparkle. "No vessel, of any size, advertises its presence in the Depths. Gods do not advertise their presences in the Depths. I would advise utter secrecy, and no major spell use while inside. As the ship is damaged, our dampening wards are weaker than they should be. If some stray magic were to leak out...."

"We'd be like a beacon." Now it was my turn to shudder. "We'll be careful, and I'll pass the word. As long as people keep to controlled areas of the ship we should be fine."

"Thank you, Officer." Guardian gave a staff sparkle, then disappeared, though it occurred to me he could hear everything and so was still present in a way.

I focused on the *Word*, on feeling through its sensors. I studied the system around us, the trade moon, and the Vagrant Fleet, and the pitiful fleet that had survived Kemet's destruction. We were so few now.

I noted that those ships had slaved their navigation to our public beacon, a standard protocol that had existed long before Kemet. It allowed ships to follow each other through the Umbral Depths, in theory. Once we were in the black, if they got off course nothing would save them. We wouldn't even know about it until we turned our sensors back on.

"Okay." I tapped all three *void* sigils and maneuvered

the vessel to the umbral shadow behind the trade moon. "Here goes."

I willed the *Word* to create a Fissure, and the vessel responded with a spell I'd heard described countless times. None of the descriptions, none of the holo episodes, none of the games did it justice.

A hellish purple glow began at the deepest part of the black. Then a fracture broke reality, like a magical hammer that had thudded into a stone wall, and sent cracks spiderwebbing through it.

It veined across the black, the glow illuminating the break. In that moment I understood what the term Fissure meant. The break in reality descended into pure blackness. Darkness so imminent and total that only in that instant did I realize I'd never known true lightlessness. Not like this.

The break I'd created was wide enough for the *Word*, so I guided us between the jagged purple breaks, and tried not to study them too closely. Looking at them riled up the shadows lurking in my mind after the Web of Divinity.

The fleet drifted in our wake, but once we passed through I lost sight of them. I keyed in the sequence I'd seen countless times to power down the all non-essential systems, and to activate the protective net of wards that would cloak us from anything capable of seeing in darkness.

The whole thing was rather anticlimactic. I pointed us on the course I'd been given, accelerated to speed, then stopped and relaxed. My work was over for the next three days, though mom had been pretty clear she wanted me here for a full twelve hours. Did I have enough books with me?

No, but I had knowledge scales. I'd been wanting to go over the haul we'd gotten from the flame. I still hadn't categorized everything.

"This place unnerves me," Vee whispered. She took a step closer to the matrix, the creaking of the ship our only accompaniment. "I know you've been touched by the *void*. I know this ship has. I know that Inura worked with Xal to build it...and I know that Inura is the Maker. I know that...that he isn't who or what I thought he was."

I considered a response, but sometimes a silent nod is the very best response you can offer.

"How do you feel about Miri?" Vee moved to stand in front of me, blinking at me with those emerald eyes. "I see you looking at her."

"Wow." I ducked out of the matrix. I wouldn't need to touch anything for days, and I wanted to sit down for this. I moved to the hovercouches along the far wall, and lounged into one. All of a sudden I understood why they were there. For bored pilots.

Vee joined me. I still searched for words.

"Listen, I know I've looked at her. She's pretty." I squirmed uncomfortably as I sought a position with back support. This thing was made for amoebas. "She's smart, and competent too. Those are good things, and I can't say with certainly there's no chemistry. But I haven't spent any time with her. For everything I like there's something I don't. She was cruel to you, and I've seen it before. Poverty does that to people. We're all trying to find our place in the pecking order."

"At others' expense." Vee's neck flushed, and the smile evaporated. "She's good at what she does, but she isn't a good person. Not really. I think she's an asset to the crew, but...Jerek, be careful. I know I don't own you, but—"

"We should go on a date sometime," I blurted, then instantly wished I could have the words back. Ah, well, may as well commit. "I don't know where things are going with us, but I like you, Vee. I like your mind. I like that you build things that save my life. I like that you have faith in people. Maybe a little too much."

The flush spread to Vee's cheeks, and she refused to look at me. "I'd like that. We can talk about details tomorrow. I'm going to go finish my bracelet, and print it if the specs line up. Maybe I can show it to you on our...date."

Then she bolted from the bridge faster than she'd ever done in the field, and I let her go without another word. I didn't want to press my luck. A date. Something to spend the next eleven and a half hours thinking about while I waited for mom to relieve me.

I couldn't help but grin.

That grin faded when the temperature dropped a good fifteen degrees. Everyone knew what that meant. It happened around spirits. I tensed and eased Dez from her holster as I sought the source of the change.

"Guardian, can you detect anything on the bridge? A presence?" I spun in a slow circle with Dez clutched in both hands. Something was here, though activating my vision didn't reveal it.

"Jerek," a low wind hissed, just at the edge of hearing. "It's Dad. Your father. This is costing me a lot of effort, so you'd best appreciate what I'm accomplishing here."

How do you react to that? Either my dead father was reaching out to me from beyond the grave, or someone was trying to impersonate him. I decided to play along and see where it led.

A shimmering fog billowed out of empty space, and coalesced into a wispy version of my dad...with legs. He stood a millimeter taller than me, which I'd never had a chance to see in life.

I knew it wasn't him. It couldn't he him. I'm pretty good at magical theory. I learned fast. We'd paid a price in bringing Seket to the present. That cost had been my father. Him, and his soul, sacrificed to the past. Ten thousand years ago...part of another time.

"You don't believe me." He rolled his eyes and drew a misty sidearm from his holster. "I have Ariela back, or a version anyway."

"Uh huh." I stifled a yawn. I needed about seventy-three more hours sleep before I felt human again. "I'm sure this isn't a trick, and you're not sent by some necromancer trying to lure me into a trap, or trying to use sentiment to extort information about this ship. It's tacky. Are you something left behind? Some sort of memory shade they fired with their cannon?"

"I didn't come with the cannon, Jer." My father folded wispy arms, the pistol resting against his opposite forearm in the trademark stance he'd spread across the planet for three years running. "A necromancer did send me. I'm not a fake. They found me on the *Flame*, Jer. Ten thousand years ago. Not long after the war that broke the fleet Necrotis took over, and started looting the other ships. She captured material, magic, souls...whatever she needed. No one else was in a position to do it. She captured me."

I didn't answer immediately. I wanted to dismiss it. There were holes I could poke, though he'd had the right answers so far.

"Anyway, her son, a guy you know by the name of Utred." Wispy dad spit a gob of smoke at the ground. "He bound me. I've been carried in a vial, just like one of them souls that kid carried around. What was his name? Vee's brother. The one with the beard. Been a long time since I thought about him."

It all sounded authentic, enough that powerful longing for my father swelled in me. Was there some hope I could help him? No, I knew that was impossible.

"Why did the necromancer send you?" Utred's game had already begun wearing on me, but I had a feeling I'd be playing it for some time.

"If you don't come to Sanctuary," my father explained in that mission-briefing way of his, "then I'll be forged into a weapon. Utred will use that weapon to kill you, and drink your soul, and then he'll do the same to your mother. He says you know he can do it. He says that if you do come, then you have a chance to stop Necrotis. They're trying to unearth a facility. Something that's been locked away for a long time. They can't get inside. They think that you can."

"Me?" Scornful laugher rolled out of me. "And you're the leverage? Dad, even if this is on the level you know I can't help these people get access to anything they might use as a weapon. I'm sorry."

"I know." His shoulders fell. "The next invitation will

be less friendly, I gather. I love you, son. Tell your sister, and your mother, that I went down swinging. I'll never betray you...any of you...I swear it."

Wispy dad evaporated, and left me with some very troubling thoughts. You might think that meant I'd put off the date.

Nah. I couldn't think of anyone better than Vee to discuss my dad's return with. Just as soon as we reached Shaya I was taking a little R&R, and Vee and I were going to spend some time doing whatever the depths we wanted.

Necromancers, politicians, and needy captains could could go diddle themselves for a day or three. I just needed to hold out until we got there.

Three days in the black may as well have been three weeks. Mom's insistence that I spend twelve hours on the bridge meant I had almost no time to myself, so I adapted in the best kind of way.

I wiled away my days learning and studying. At the noon hour Vee would pop by with lunch, and she'd show me what she'd been working on. Today was the day she'd be presenting her bracelet. The last day. The day we arrived at Shaya.

Briff, Rava, Miri, Seket, and Kurz all kept to the *Remora*, though Vee kept me apprised of their activities, which mostly consisted of Arena games and much needed sleep.

The door to the bridge hissed open and I looked up from the knowledge scale I'd been studying. This particular one detailed the Catalysts in our sector. There were so many I'd never heard of, and at least some must still exist. Someday I'd write a history of the Catalysts that had changed since the account I was reading.

"Morning." Vee offered a cheerful smile as she approached with a basket, and dropped into a crouch next to the matrix. "I brought coffee this time. Your mother loves the stuff, and it's really growing on me. We never had access shipboard, and I wasn't allowed anywhere that sold it when we were planetside."

"Thanks." I accepted the cup she passed me, and inhaled, though it was still too hot to drink. "None of the others could make it?"

"No." Vee blushed again. "I mean, I didn't try that hard. They're on day three of their Arena league, and were pretty much all yelling at their respective holos. Even Miri is playing, though I think she's just looking for something to do. She had that bored air about her. If it had been anyone but me leaving the ship she'd have offered to go I think. If she knew I was meeting you, I bet she'd have come even knowing it meant spending time with me."

"Well, I'm happy you did come." I inhaled deeply. "Lunch smells amazing. Thank you, Ternus, for the genetic schematics to that heavenly creature."

I missed Briff the most, but I knew they'd earned the time off. I wish I could share it. But the odds of me having research time in the next month were slim to none, and I'd used it well. It had helped heal something inside me, and I felt much more ready to face whatever we'd find at Shaya.

Theoretically, it would be a paradise that would offer us sanctuary, but when did things ever play out like I thought they would? I was fully prepared to be fired upon when we arrived, or have some equally dangerous threat appear without warning. There was still my father's shade to deal with, which I hadn't brought up to Vee yet.

"So when are we arriving?" Vee opened the basket and removed a truly massive slab of ground beef pressed between a thick bun. She passed it to me, and I began salivating.

"Three minutes." I paused to devour about a third of the burger. My first meal since I'd started my shift. "At least...if my coordinates are right. If not...well, let's not think about that."

I continued to eat in silence, and she did the same. That was one of the things I really enjoyed about Vee. We could share a comfortable silence.

"Okay, here goes." I rose to my feet and tapped all three *void* sigils. "Let's hope my math was right." There was almost zero chance of it being wrong, and had it been I'm certain Guardian would have pointed it out. I still worried.

I keyed the *void* sigils again, this time to initiate the Fissure. Reality split once more, but this time from the other side. My eyes burned as a brilliant blue-green world filled the scry-screen, the entire planet carpeted in trees and oceans.

The term Great Tree made instant sense when I saw how large a few of the trees were. They towered over the rest of the world, stabbing up into orbit. Entire cities dotted some of their branches, especially on the tree directly beneath the planet's umbral shadow.

Countless firefly lights gave the dark side of the world definition below, though I noted they only touched a few of the trees. Much of the planet appeared to be untouched wilderness, an impossibility back on Kemet where every kilo was owned and parceled.

It might have been the most beautiful thing I'd ever seen, and that was before you took in the mighty fleet in orbit, the glittering golden ships, and stations, all hovering over the largest tree. A few of the ships had even been constructed from wood. That seemed impossible, but there it was. Who constructed a starship out of wood?

"You were going to show me that bracelet." I turned to Vee, the planet forgotten. It was cool and all, but I'd been waiting days to see this eldimagus she'd designed. The artistry that had gone into the components took my breath, and I'd spent hours listening to her explain how it all worked.

Vee raised her left arm absently to show off the bracelet, though her eyes were still on Shaya, wide and focused. The light made them shine, and her smile made it perfect.

I glanced away hurriedly before she caught me. Something to focus on....

The bracelet had been forged from a gold alloy, twined with a pale silver one, so fine it could pass for white. I recognized neither, but the diamonds pulsed with *life*, and the sapphires with *water*.

"It's designed to enhance protection and nature spells," I realized aloud. "I'm impressed."

"It's just a journeyman's piece." Vee nudged me through the matrix's rings and nodded at Shaya below us. "You can look at the bracelet whenever. This is the first time we're seeing a whole other world. One filled with magic, and trees, and...air. Look at this place."

As the Fissure snapped shut in our wake, the sun glinted off a ship I hadn't noticed, one hovering above the rest of the fleet. The only vessel in the system that rivaled the *Word of Xal* in size.

The golden ship stretched out over the planet like a staff discarded by a god, its long slender length gleaming in the light of the sun, but also providing its own brilliant luminance.

"The *Spellship*," I murmured, unaware I'd spoken aloud until Vee replied.

"Yeah." She pushed a lock of hair out of her eyes. It was the first time I realized she'd been wearing it loose instead of the usual ponytail. I liked it. "I watched a documentary about the Ternus purification campaign. Most of it is classified, but they talked about Lady Voria and the *Spellship*. I guess it was pivotal in many of the battles that reshaped the sector."

My mind strayed to Ardaki, the staff that Guardian had told me was connected to the *Spellship*. Some sort of key. A fact that I might be the only one aware of, outside of Inura himself. So many troubling questions.

A cold thrum washed through me as I felt an incoming missive from the *Spellship*. I accepted and the *Spellship*'s bridge filled my scry-screen.

I don't know who I expected. Lady Voria, maybe. A god. An official in a uniform covered in medals. What I got was an unassuming man a few years older than Rava, with an easy smile, a sea of freckles, and an infectious disposition.

"Hey, there, *Word of Xal*. My name is Administrator Pickus." He delivered a bucktoothed smile, which did nothing to detract from his authority. "I run day-to-day operations for the fleet, and for the *Spellship*. We've been told to expect your arrival. The pantheon will be in session shortly, but after they're finished I'm sure they'll wish to speak to you, or the current captain of the vessel."

That last had the ring of a question.

"My mother, Irala, is who you'll be dealing with." It sounded as awkward as I'd feared. "I'll have her contact you as soon as she's available. The journey here has been...trying. We have wights and worse infesting the ship, and a lot of half-trained kids having to grow up very quickly."

"From what I hear you aren't kids any more." Pickus offered a salute, hand over heart. "Sit tight. You're safe now. We'll leave what comes next in the hands of the gods, but if you need anything in the meantime don't hesitate to ask. I handle logistics, so medicine, life mages, food, materials for forges...we can make sure you have anything you need."

I had to admit that it felt like a trap even though I knew he couldn't lie to me. This guy believed what he was saying, to the core. Yet I'd been burned. Often. It was so hard to trust.

"Thank you, Pickus." I rolled my neck, thankful my shift would be over soon and this would be Mom's problem. "We appreciate the confederate aid."

"Course. Y'all get some rest." He nodded and the missive ended.

I decided to take his advice. Sure, I'd had a night's sleep. But I needed about twenty more.

"Hey, I know it's lunch time." Where had my burger

gone? Had I really devoured it without being aware of it? "But I think I'm going to go grab a nap."

Everything we'd been through crushed me to the deck, a sudden weariness that I couldn't repress any longer.

"Do you want company?" Her smile said we probably wouldn't get much sleep.

Suddenly, heroically, I found an inner reservoir of strength I hadn't known I possessed. "No, I don't take naps with beautiful girls. If you want to come with me you can try to change my mind on the way though."

"Boobs."

"Touche." I stifled a mock yawn. "All right, let's nap."

Interlude VII

When Inura translocated to the coordinates he'd been provided he expected a trap. He performed none of his usual auguries. He did nothing to alter his fate or seek advantage. Inura was tired. So tired. If this was the end, then let it come, and come swiftly.

The pantheon that awaited him sat in judgement around a flat stone table that had been carved long before any of them had been born. He didn't recognize the world, though he wasn't one to value any specific one. The young gods lounged with warm mugs in their hands, and both Aran and Kheross were laughing. So young.

Inura didn't know the white-haired demigod well, but Kheross had always struck him as a stoic Wyrm. Laughter seemed out of place, though he preferred it to the usual glower.

Lady Voria sat at the center of the bench running next to the table, somehow more regal than the rest of them. Her chestnut hair shone, and complimented her understated uniform.

Xal'Aran, the newly minted demon prince, turned in his direction as he laughed, and Inura caught sight of the fangs. The handsome purple-skinned demon reminded him so much of Xal. Too much. More and more Inura suspected the elder god's direct hand.

Xal operated well beyond the rest of them. He'd been an immortal longer than recorded history, and history had been recorded for a very, very long time.

Did Aran understand what he was? What he represented? None of Xal lurked there. The body might be the same, but the mind was entirely new. Xal's consciousness must be elsewhere, leaving Inura to wonder at the genetic double. What did Xal play at? Was there a master plan, or simply an attempt at offspring?

If not for another being in the room Inura might have investigated further. Voria didn't sit alone. Her right hand wrapped firmly around the haft of a golden staff Inura had labored upon for decades. Ikadra, the first key.

The gleaming sunsteel shone, and the sapphire near the tip pulsed as the weapon whispered no doubt sage counsel to its owner.

"You have invited me and I have come," Inura intoned, in a manner befitting gods. "I submit myself to the judgement of your pantheon, and if you are willing, seek to join your covenant."

He considered making a case for his petition, but sensed it might be premature, so he left it there. Let them decide where to take the conversation. There was certainly a great deal to discuss.

"Dad!" Ikadra's sapphire pulsed as the staff thrummed with joy. "You're alive. Oh, my god, you're alive. You must owe so much back child support. I don't think there's a statute of limitations for immortals, and you sired a loooooot of kids...not just me. Oh...I get it. That's why you faked your death. To dodge alimony and child support and what not. I think you kind of blew it by coming to the Confederacy, bud."

Inura scarcely knew how to respond to a normal god, but this was...he ignored the key, which had clearly been warped by one or more previous owners. Shaya, if he were to guess. Entrusting her with the staff had been the right move, but the cost....

"Welcome, Inura." Voria rose from her seat, and performed a Confederate salute. "I understand you have a case to present about recent events in the Kemet system. Is it true that an entire trade moon has been wiped out?"

"You're a goddess now." Inura rolled his eyes, unable to stifle the irritation. This woman had vexed him at every turn, despite owing much of her power directly to him. "The answer to that is a glimpse of divinity away."

"I see." Voria's mouth firmed into a tight, unforgiving line. "Inura, may I be candid with you today?"

Inura sensed he'd overstepped his bounds, but stiffened and refused to bow to the storm about to break over him. "Of course. If I am to petition for membership, then some very...harsh questions are likely to be asked."

"Membership?" A blond man Inura didn't recognize raised an eyebrow. His drawl put him from Ternus.

"Name's Davidson. As I understand it we're not a club, and we ain't a superhero team. Each of us represents the government of a world or nation who signed a very specific treaty. Which world do you represent, Inura? What exactly are you the god of? 'Cause I don't see you anywhere on the Confederate charter."

The man possessed a bit of *water* magic, but was otherwise a mortal, with a paltry handful of decades. Inura found it disturbing that he even had a place at this table. The mistake was his, though. He'd assumed their laws would function as other pantheons had, but clearly they'd made their own.

"Forgive me." Inura performed an elegant bow, made easier by the fact that he gave it to a man who looked so similar to his mentor, Xal. "Each pantheon I have known rose from a previous. At least one surviving god passed on the traditions that preceded them, as a common form of language between deities. Should you venture to another reality or galaxy, then it helps to share some common ground. I must remind myself that the Confederacy is a governing body, not a pantheon as I know it."

The one called Davidson sat, and savored a mouthful of that foul smelling bean drink they all seemed to love. They drank it hot, too, for some reason.

"Respectfully," Voria snapped, her eyes aflame with her divinity, "you do not have the floor, Inura. We have not recognized you. You are a guest. We need to know what happened in that system. We need to know if these necromancers are a threat. Who are they? Why are they appearing now? We need to know if the other Great Ships can be salvaged. We have many questions. Please, why don't you begin with what you discovered in the Kemet system?"

"You don't want to know how I survived?" Inura hated how petulant he sounded, but there it was.

"No." Frit rose to her feet, the fire goddess easily the most powerful deity in the room. "No one cares. Let's deal with the current business so I can get back to mine. I don't have time for old-god drama."

"I care." Aran rose to his feet, and met Frit stare for stare. There was no love lost there, though Aran subsided when Nara placed a hand on his forearm. He turned to Inura. "It was my spell that disintegrated Inura. Yet here you stand. Diminished, but alive. You bear no touch of Xal, or I'd feel you. How did you do whatever you did?"

"I am a shade," he explained, without preamble or embellishment. "I placed my consciousness in this body, and gifted it with a large reservoir of *life* magic. In short, I cut off a small appendage and placed myself in it. I am weak. Pitifully weak. But all my knowledge and experience, all my artificing expertise, those things still exist. You are a newly anointed pantheon on the eve of a war that will dwarf anything that has come during your brief reign. The unseen fleets are not like other threats."

"And, pray tell, what are they like?" Voria's tone carried her weariness.

"You wanted my account. I will give it." Inura straightened his posture, and reminded himself that he was the eldest here, whatever their relative strengths. It was his role to pass on knowledge they needed. "I have been in the Kemet system surveying the Great Ships. I spent time on each, enough to see that none will be so easy to claim as the *Word*. The ships lack magic, but they are populated by entire nations in some cases. During my survey I discovered a necromancer who claims to be my daughter aboard the *Inura's Grace*. Necrotis found a way to murder the ship and raise it as the *Maker's Wrath*. It is a tool for war now. One we should fear."

"Did the trade moon really fall to a single shot?" Aran's hand dropped to his side where he rested it on the hilt of a potent eldimagus blade, a gesture one would expect from a mortal, but not a god.

"Worse," Inura countered. "A single shot killed everyone on that moon, without harming any of the tech. Necrotis sent down dozens of transports with skilled necromancers. Those necromancers are converting every soul on that moon into an army of incredible size. If not for the actions of a few heroes, the boy Jerek and his companions, that moon would be the gravest threat this sector has faced since Nefarius. As it stands that system belongs to our enemies. If they reinforce that moon with the other Great Ships there will be no stopping them."

"You mentioned unseen fleets." Nara's quiet voice drew all eyes. The demoness still looked more human than demon, but her wings and horns were growing. "What are they and how do they link to this Necrotis?"

"We come to the heart of it." Inura bowed his head. "One of the gravest threats overcome by the dragonflights were the unseen fleets. Back then *spirit* magic, and necrotech, were much more common. The unseen fleets trace their lineage back to the exodus from the Great Cycle, and at one time controlled most of this galaxy. The Wyrmmother, my mother, brought the dragonflights to break their grip on these systems. Doing so required all eight flights, and many allies, such as Xal and his offspring. Even Krox saw the need, despite being of *spirit* himself. He profited greatly from those wars, and absorbed many of their lesser gods."

Inura raised his head, and let his gaze roam them. He had them all then. Every set of eyes had locked on him, and they patiently awaited his next words.

"The name unseen arose after we broke their power." Inura's eyes misted as he remembered back to his youth, his very first war. "We wrested the secrets of binding and necromancy, and the spirit realm from them. Only the unseen, those necromancers wise enough to avoid attention could hope to survive. We found and killed the rest, and called it justice. Those who escaped our extermination retreated to hidden corners of the galaxy. The largest enclave lies in this sector, which is why a goddess as powerful as Virkonna was charged with watching over it. You'd know it as Sanctuary, the raging storm. It covers a full light year, and within that mess lurk the unseen fleets. No one knows how many, or even what Catalysts are contained there. Not even gods do more than skirt the edges."

"So you're telling me," Aran interjected in a clear voice that captured all eyes, "that they've been patiently building up their forces while the sector tore itself apart? I don't need to ask why this Necrotis is making her move now. She's doing it now because we're in disarray. We need to do something about the remaining Great Ships."

"What about Sanctuary itself?" Frit asked, concern

etched on her youthful features. "Should we establish an outpost? I can ask my flame readers to scry it."

"Investigating would seem prudent," Voria allowed, the first time she'd offered an opinion, Inura noted. Smart. "However, we are stretched thin and ill prepared to deal with a new threat. I'd recommend we focus our efforts on recovering the remaining Great Ships."

"I'd agree." Aran nodded.

"Likewise." Davidson savored another sip of bean juice. "We can't police a storm that these people already control. We can retrofit more warships, and get ready for a brawl if they decide they want one."

Relief crept into Inura's gut, but he smothered it, denying the flame oxygen. They hadn't done anything yet. This was all still just talk. If they took no action, then by the time they were prepared to deal with the unseen it would be far too late.

But they wanted to help. They wanted to protect. They wanted to improve the galaxy. Hope, in spite of all his best attempts, sprouted in fertile soil.

EPILOGUE

I leaned back into luxurious pillows, and enjoyed the bed's soft silk against my legs while I struggled to catch my breath. It was damned good to be out of the armor, even if briefly. And it was damned good to have lovely company.

"You didn't tell me it was your first time." Vee wrapped a comforting arm around me, and gave my shoulder a squeeze. "Two minutes isn't really that bad."

I tried not to let her sympathy at my abysmal performance irk me. I hated being bad at things I enjoyed, though. Hated it.

"Here, give it to me. I'll show you how." She gave an inviting smile that eased the sting of the words. "You just need practice is all. I'm happy to teach you."

"Fine." I handed her the controller with my most petulant sigh. "Do not tell Briff. He will never, not ever, stop griefing me about this."

I focused on the holoscreen in the corner, which displayed a game very much different than Arena.

Kem'Kem was a puzzler where different colored scales rained from the top of the screen. You had to arrange them with incredible precision, or they piled up until they reached the top and you lost.

Be honest. You thought I was talking about something else, didn't you? Get your mind out of the gutter.

"You sure you don't want to play something else?" I sighed as she perfectly controlled the flow of pieces onto the screen, while looking in my direction.

"Sure, after I beat this level. Anything but Aren—". Her smile died as she focused on something behind me.

A distant buzzing in my head preceded the cold fire that rammed into my side, under the ribs. I didn't realize a knife had caused the damage until the blade struck bone, and the assassin withdrew it for another attempt, warm blood spurting down my back.

My elbow shot out with all the force I could manage, and my aim was true. It slammed into the assassin's gut, which knocked the breath from him, and loosened his hold on the dagger. At least it meant he breathed.

I focused on my magic, and cast a blink spell to the far side of the room. The assassin spun in place, my blood dripping from the dagger that he'd ripped loose when I'd ported as he struggled to locate me.

Vee stepped in front of me, and snapped down her new bracelet. A brilliant swirl of blue-white sigils wound out of it to form a large shield, which she held protectively before the both of us.

Vee's aura flared, and the golden light of the Maker's blessing drew tendrils of smoke from the assassin's armored form. The damage seemed superficial, but the would-be assassin retreated a step, into the holo display, the happy music running counterpoint to his panting as brightly colored scales swirled around him.

That gave me enough of a gap to snatch Dez from her holster near the nightstand. I took a moment to steady my aim, and I cast a good old dream bolt. I'd already seen how effective it could be.

Warm pink energy filled the barrel, and my weapon discharged into the assassin's face. I considered a second shot, my go-to normally, but having *life* magic changed my priorities. I was bleeding out.

I placed Dez's barrel against my side, and willed the flesh to knit back together. Warm golden energy flowed to the effected area, and the pain abated, though not entirely. The wound refused to heal, and I could feel something unnatural lingering there.

"My work is done," the assassin hissed, unfazed by my spell. "This vessel means nothing."

His entire body began to thrash wildly, and a thin silver cloud rose from his mouth. The body slumped over, discarded like a Ternus MRE container as the cloud dissipated into nothing.

"Vee?" I clutched at my kidney, and gritted my chest against the cold. "Something's not right about the wound."

Vee lunged across the bed, and pressed me onto my stomach to inspect the wound. Another wave of warm golden energy washed through me, and relief loosened my muscles, but once the spell stopped the strange knot returned.

"It's still there." I probed the skin, which had healed.

"We'll need to get someone here to look at it. I'm told Shayan doctors are the best in the sector."

"Why do they want you dead?" Vee prodded the assassin's body with her foot.

"They don't." I groaned my way into a sitting position. It wasn't painful, exactly, but something still felt off. "I don't know what they're playing at."

A shimmering cloud of unclean vapor began spraying from my ear, and I temporarily lost hearing on that side. I cupped it, unable to stem the tide as smoke flowed out of me.

The vapor pooled into a meter-tall figure not unlike the version of my father that had visited me on the bridge. Only this wasn't my dad. This was an Inuran. One I was coming to know far better than I'd like.

"Utred." I gripped Dez with both hands. "I don't know what your game is, but I'm already tired of playing. What did you do to me?"

"I merely offered a little incentive." Phantom Utred delivered a pleasant smile. "I wanted to ensure you were fully aware of the stakes, and now I can communicate with you regardless of distance. Congratulations. You have acquired a very rare piece of necrotech. Or necroware to be more precise, not unlike the cyberware your sister favors. Anyway, enough about me. How did your visit with your father's spirit go?"

"Jer?" Vee still stood before me, her aura blindingly hot as it enveloped the room. "Should we attack this thing? He's spewing nothing but lies."

"Not so far it isn't." I shook my head. "I don't know what his game is, like I said, but I can tell you that he's not lying. What do you want, Utred? You wanted to communicate? We're communicating."

"Come to Sanctuary." Utred's smile grew mischievous. "You and I are going to do something no one expects. Deep in the storm lies a facility that predates the up-jumped lizards who conquered this sector. That facility is, unfortunately, hostile to the unliving. We are incinerated on sight. Only a mortal can even approach, much less find a way inside. An exceedingly clever mortal."

"So how does this play out? I head inside, gain control, and turn over a mega-powerful research facility to you? Something that can easily overpower the *Word of Xal*, probably. That's not an arms race I want to get involved in." I rubbed my kidney, which still had an ice cube lodged inside.

"That's one possibility." Utred's smile undulated in a sinister way. "Or you could seize the facility for yourself."

"I already have a Great Ship," I pointed out. "What need do I have for super powerful factory? And why do you want me to have it?"

"This isn't merely a factory. This is a conduit. It was built *inside* the Great Cycle. Jerek, we can not only learn where we came from, but maybe get back to the paradise we were originally exiled from. Tell me you don't want to know where we all originally came from. How all this started."

Taking Utred seriously took some work, but the ice cube lent weight to his arguments. The kind of knowledge a facility that old might hold...it had probably been created by an entirely different species. It would fill in a massive gap in our history. Maybe even learn about the beginning of everything, a question that haunted scholars. No one had any real idea how old the universe was. I hated to admit it, but the idea tempted me far more than it should have.

"No, thanks. I already have plenty of reading to catch up on." I held up the current knowledge scale I was studying. "The knowledge isn't quite so old, but it's a lot safer than flying into a death storm and meeting you and your buddies. I get what you get if I were to locate this ship. I don't get what might incentivize me to help you. I mean, in spite of the free necroware, I still don't trust you, for some reason."

"Very well." Utred gave a deeply exaggerated sigh. "If you refuse to help I will be forced to transform your father into a reaper, one of our pet assassins. I will pick one of your loved ones at random, and your father will kill them. Each day you refuse to head to Sanctuary he will be forced to kill someone else that he loves. Is that really what you want for your father?"

The fact that I knew he wasn't lying chilled me more than the ice cube ever could. He really had my father, and would really turn him into the same type of assassin who'd attempted to kill my mother, and who'd given me my non-elective surgery.

"Can I have some time to think about it? You've been reasonable so far." I hoped I could play on his civility, which seemed important to him.

"Of course. I will come to you again in a day's time. Give it some thought. Perform auguries. Talk to gods. Whatever you wish...but if I return and the answer is still no? Well, your father will pay the price, Jerek. I'm sorry for that." Utred's tone expressed either genuine regret, or an amazing imitation. "Do the smart thing, Jerek. We can still be allies. There is no need for war between our people. Come to Sanctuary, and I will tell you all about this facility. We only want one specific artifact inside of it. The discovery could make your career, and give you the power to stop nasty people such as myself."

The smoke dissipated dramatically, then melted into the floor. I released a breath I hadn't realized I'd been holding. Part of me had feared it would slither back into my ear.

What the depths was I going to do now?

THE MAGITECH CHRONICLES
CHARACTER SHEET

NAME: Jerek

RACE: Human

ARCHETYPE: True Mage

PATH: Relic Hunter

HIT POINTS		SPELL POINTS		INITIATIVE
20	20	21	21	3(6)

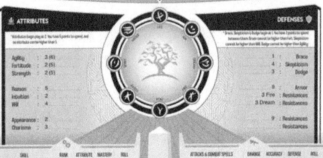

⚗ ATTRIBUTES

Attributes begin play at 2. You have 6 points to spend, and no attribute can be higher than 5.

Agility	:	3 (6)
Fortitude	:	2 (5)
Strength	:	2 (5)
Reason	:	5
Intuition	:	2
Will	:	4
Appearance	:	2
Charisma	:	3

DEFENSES 🛡

Brace, Skepticism & Dodge begin at 1. You have 3 points to spend between them. Brace cannot be higher than Fort. Skepticism cannot be higher than Will. Dodge cannot be higher than Agility.

1	:	Brace
4	:	Skepticism
3	:	Dodge
8	:	Armor
3 Fire	:	Resistances
3 Dream	:	Resistances
9	:	Resistances
	:	Resistances

SKILL	RANK	ATTRIBUTE	MASTERY	ROLL
Spellcasting	3	5	N	8
Arcana	4	5	Y	9
History and Lore	5	5	Y	10
Perception	3	2	Y	5
Ranged	4	3/5	Y	9
Negotiation	3	3	N	6

ATTACKS & COMBAT SPELLS	DAMAGE	ACCURACY	DEFENSE	ROLL
Heka Aten Fire Bolt	4/3	2	SKEP	10
Heka Aten Void Bolt	5	3	SKEP	11

ARMOR	A/B	EFFECT
Heka Aten Spellarmor	9/9	

ABILITIES & SPELLS	EFFECT
Decipher	Translate any language
Tomb Robber	Edge when using eldimagus
Dream Bolt	
Fire Bolt	
Invest Strength	
Invest Charisma	
Perfect Perception	Cannot be lied to. Always see.

SPECIALIZATION	ASPECT	BENEFIT
Fire Magic	Fire	3 pool, 3 fire resistance
Dream Magic	Dream	3 pool, 3 dream resistance
Life Magic	Life	3 Pool, 3 life resistance

PERKS	FLAWS
Slippery Molo (+1 Dodge)	Skipped Leg Day (-1 Strength)

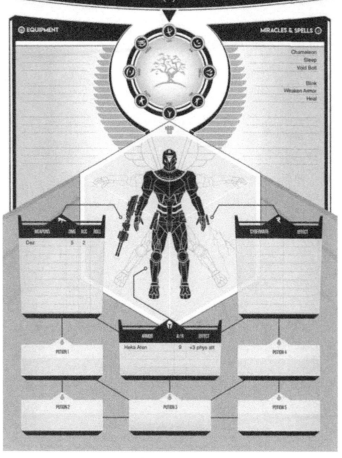

THE MAGITECH CHRONICLES
CHARACTER SHEET

EQUIPMENT

MIRACLES & SPELLS

Chameleon
Sleep
Void Bolt

Blink
Weaken Armor
Heal

WEAPONS	DMG	ACC	ROLL
Daz	5	2	

CYBERWARE	EFFECT

ARMOR	A/R	EFFECT
Heka Aten	9	+3 phys att

POTION 1

POTION 4

POTION 2

POTION 3

POTION 5

Note to the Reader

If you enjoyed *Necrotech*, we have a complete seven-book prequel series with an ending already available, and it leads seamlessly into the book you just read.

Our pen & paper RPG successfully Kickstarted and the game will be live on July 30th, 2020. You can learn more by signing up to the mailing list, or visit magitechchronicles.com and our Magitech Chronicles World Anvil page.

We've got maps, lore, character sheets, and a free set of rules you can use to generate your own character, plus a Facebook group where we geek out about this stuff.

I hope you enjoy and we can't wait to meet you! If you have any trouble finding what you need email me at chris@chrisfoxwrites.com and I'll get you sorted.

-Chris

Printed in Great Britain
by Amazon

25982615R00145